SABOTAGE

DALE WILEY

Best Wishes

VESUVIAN BOOKS

Los Angeles   New York   Nashville

Sabotage

This is a work of fiction. Names, characters, places, and incidents either are the product of the author's imagination or are used fictitiously. Any resemblance to actual persons, living or dead, events or locales is entirely coincidental.

ISBN: 978-1-944109-04-2 (print)
ISBN: 978-1-944109-05-9 (ebook)

Published by Vesuvian Books
www.vesuvianbooks.com

Printed in the United States of America

10 9 8 7 6 5 4 3 2 1

To Mary, Sara, and Matt, who fill my life every day with adventure and love.

To Candice and Mackenzie, for friendship beyond compare.

Other Books by Dale Wiley

The Intern
Kissing Persuasive Lips

Coming Soon

Southern Gothic
The Jefferson Bible

TABLE OF CONTENTS

One 1

Two 8

Three 15

Four 20

Five 25

Six... 28

Seven 34

Eight.. 37

Nine 40

Ten.. 46

Eleven 50

Twelve 55

Thirteen.. 57

Fourteen 60

Fifteen 64

Sixteen... 67

Seventeen 70

Eighteen... 73

Nineteen... 76

Twenty 80

Twenty-One 83

Twenty-Two.. 91

Twenty-Three 94

Twenty-Four... 97

Twenty-Five... 100

Twenty-Six 103

Twenty-Seven 105

Twenty-Eight... 110

Twenty-Nine 113

Thirty 115

Thirty-One 118

Thirty-Two.. 121
Thirty-Three.. 123
Thirty-Four... 125
Thirty-Five.. 130
Thirty-Six... 133
Thirty-Seven.. 135
Thirty-Eight... 138
Thirty-Nine.. 143
Forty.. 146
Forty-One... 150
Forty-Two... 154
Forty-Three.. 156
Forty-Four.. 159
Forty-Five... 161
Forty-Six.. 162
Forty-Seven.. 163
Forty-Eight... 169
Forty-Nine.. 172
Fifty... 175
Fifty-One.. 177
Fifty-Two... 180
Fifty-Three... 184
Fifty-Four... 187
Fifty-Five... 190
Fifty-Six.. 193
Fifty-Seven.. 196
Fifty-Eight... 199
Fifty-Nine.. 204
Sixty.. 206
Sixty-One... 208
Sixty-Two... 210
Sixty-Three.. 213
Sixty-Four.. 214
Sixty-Five... 216
Sixty-Six.. 218

Sixty-Seven 220
Sixty-Eight 223
Sixty-Nine 225
Seventy 228
Seventy-One 230
Seventy-Two 233
Seventy-Three 235
Seventy-Four 238
Seventy-Five 240
Seventy-Six 242
Seventy-Seven 244
Seventy-Eight 246
Seventy-Nine 247
Eighty 249
Eighty-One 251
Eighty-Two 253
Eighty-Three 256
Eighty-Four 259
Eighty-Five 262
Eighty-Six 264
Epilogue 267

ONE

The money, all forty thousand dollars, was lined up on the counter when Seth got there.

It might as well have been a million to Seth. He was used to big deals but that was when the economy was good, and people threw money around for fun. He did too, back then. Then everything changed, and the money people, even in Vegas, went into their holes and stopped sharing. This was important and different and better. And it came at the right time, too.

The deal worked like this: he got to leave with half the cash—twenty thousand dollars—right then. He rented a safe-deposit box to keep it in; that was the first time he had been in a bank in years. Yes, this was risky, but he got to leave with that unthinkable amount of money this morning. He would spend one hour on a plane, and then he was done—pretty much, anyway. And the rest of the money? His before nightfall.

He stood on the thirty-fourth floor of the Trump Tower, one

1

of the newer and more impressive addresses in Las Vegas. It was seven a.m. The sky was a warm yellow and promised heat, like almost every day in Vegas, but he didn't get to see it much, not like this anyway. He couldn't remember when he had last been awake at this hour of the morning or, at least, when he had woken up at this time. In a town like Vegas, you often went down when the sun came up. Normally, he was either rolling in about now or sleeping off the after-effects of a long night. But an early morning was what the job required, and Seth desperately needed this.

Seth had been to this apartment several times before. He was initially wary of his benefactor's strange behavior—aloof and put-on, far from the passionate pawing of his other suitors—but he began to understand. He felt sure he was hired because he looked so much like the man who paid him so well to come and visit. It was uncanny. His own skin was a shade darker than his doppelganger, but both men were handsome, around six feet tall, dark complexion, and had dark hair with light eyes. Twice on his visits, the doorman smiled at him as if he were the building's resident. It took some getting used to, to sit across from yourself and talk, but Seth got used to things very quickly.

Seth was an escort, a plaything. He liked his job most of the time, but it led him into odd circumstances. Men paying to suck his toes. Men wanting to cut his hair. He still wasn't fully sure what to make of the quiet man who brought him here to his apartment. Most other men desired Seth's body, wanted to devour him, to come out of the closet in Vegas before stepping back in and heading home, or to add him to their strange Vegas menagerie—not Yankee. He told him he just wanted companionship and conversation, just like the ad on Seth's website said—no sex and no toe-sucking. Seth wondered if Yankee liked the idea of talking to himself, given their similarity in appearance.

Yankee's apartment, where they always met, was big and somewhat bland, looking and feeling more like a nice, big hotel suite than a real place where someone lived. Most of the men who lived in Vegas and invited him to their places loved to show off expansive and well-decorated homes, with Rothko's, Hockney's, and other tasteful paintings. The rest were festive and overdone palaces straight out of a Fellini film. Yankee's place felt like the junior suite at the nicest hotel in town but nothing more. It featured maid service and a kitchen that looked like no one ever cooked there. Seth walked by the kitchen every time he walked in, and he always took a longing look inside. Seth, who was a good and thoughtful cook, hated to see such a wonderful space wasted by someone who didn't appreciate or have time for it. He wondered how much time Yankee actually spent here.

After the third visit, when Yankee said he knew him well enough, he asked Seth if he would be interested in a big job—not just a thousand dollars here and there but a score. Yankee told him he looked into his background—or what he thought he knew of it—and felt he could be trusted. He also knew from Seth's profession he long ago lost his tendency to gag.

Yankee looked at him seriously. "Are you interested? I understand if you're not."

Of course, Seth was interested. He occasionally made good money, but there were all of the craps tables and party drugs to think about. Seth wanted to have a nest egg. He nodded and waited for what Yankee would say.

"Just swallow three condoms, filled with drugs. Take a one-hour flight. Take some laxatives and release. Make twenty thousand upon swallowing, twenty thousand upon releasing the packages back to the owners. Some chance of death, some chance of prison."

As Seth saw it, he dealt with those risks every day he sold himself in Las Vegas and for a much smaller return.

He was nervous. He sat on the stiff leather couch, which seemed like no one ever sat on, knowing Yankee would appear after what seemed like an eternity. This was his way. Seth sat and looked at the money.

He thought about just taking the money, grabbing the first elevator, and praying for ground, but he looked around and once again sensed he was being watched. He knew there was another entrance to this apartment, and he didn't know whether Yankee was already here or coming through that entrance. But he knew enough to be sure he didn't want to cross this man. Despite his kindness, Seth knew Yankee could be cruel without losing his quiet demeanor. There was always a chance that a condom would rupture in his stomach during his flight, or he would get caught by officers waiting in Los Angeles, but those risks were nothing compared with dashing away with the money. He assumed that indiscretion would assure an all but certain death. And though he might say in a fit of boy-induced drama that sometimes he wished he would die, he really didn't. He wanted this to go well, and he wanted to pocket the rewards.

Seth wondered if you could see his thoughts on the surveillance screen. He didn't want to give anything away. He didn't want to risk Yankee pulling back. He went back to thinking like a mule. That was what this job required. If he got paid this well, he would think like a mule, act like a mule, be a mule.

Finally, some fifteen minutes later, in came Yankee. He kissed Seth gently on the cheek as he always did. This was their only physical contact.

"Big day!" said Yankee in an overly fey manner. Seth knew he wasn't gay. "Are you ready?"

"I'm ready," said Seth, who had been anticipating this for weeks.

"Well, they're in the fridge." Yankee went and opened the refrigerator and took out a plate with three pink condoms on it. "I put some strawberry jam on them," Yankee said. "I know that's your fave."

The condoms were filled with a gelatinous substance. They were the size of small bananas, but not difficult to get down. At the last visit, they practiced swallowing some condoms close to this size with a similar liquid. They timed how long it took them to come out: two and a half hours. Yankee paid him double for that session.

Yankee assured him that these were double-bagged. Seth smiled and said, "Down the hatch." He opened up the back of his throat and swallowed the three packages easily, followed by lots of water.

"Lie down. Like last time," Yankee said, a little hurried. "Then I'll take you to the airport."

Seth did. This place made him sleepy anyway. He moved to the couch, took off his shoes, and laid down. He closed his eyes and relaxed.

Yankee went to the kitchen. He opened the knife drawer and took out the H&K pistol that was hidden in the back. The silencer was already on.

Seth started to drift. Then it hit him. Why would Yankee want someone who looked like him to make this run? Why wouldn't he want someone completely different? Why would he want connections?

Checking one more time to make sure Seth's eyes were closed, Yankee emerged from the kitchen. He strode stiffly across the room. Yankee bent over Seth and held his breath.

Seth felt the weight on top of his chest and opened his eyes in terror. He realized what was happening. He tried to push Yankee away but couldn't. There was no leverage. He started to yell "No," but it was too late. Yankee put the gun up to Seth's left eye and pulled the trigger. All that was heard was a sound no louder than a handclap. Seth slumped. Yankee started to shoot again but saw it was unnecessary. Seth, the greedy escort, was no more.

Yankee flipped his body off the couch and onto the floor, where he landed face-down, exactly as planned. Blood rolled down the leather couch where Seth's head lay. He took the coffee table and flipped it on top of the body, enough movement to cause papers to scatter but not enough to make much of a sound. He eased it on top of the remote-operated bomb that was now Seth the Escort. Yankee looked down and saw he managed to get some blood on himself, which was not surprising. The room, normally so neat, was now oh, such a mess. Yankee laughed. He was still playing the fake fairy.

It didn't matter. Yankee was never coming back. He took off his clothes and placed them in a black garbage bag. Just like the condoms filled with plastic explosives that now rested in Seth's belly, he double-bagged them. He turned the thermostat all the way down; he wanted it to feel like a meat locker in the apartment. Then he went into the heat and steam of the shower and took his time. Lather, rinse, repeat. Stay calm and think. He breathed deeply and fully, slowing his heart rate as best as he could, and made sure his plan was ready. He came out of the shower, put on his delivery man getup, replete with white coveralls and a red cap, put the trash bag in one hand and a clipboard in the other, and found the service elevator. He keyed in the code and rode down, happy that no one shared the ride. He made it to the ground floor and tossed the trash bag into the back of the trash truck, which backed into the bay, nodding at a couple of workers as he headed for the parking lot. He walked to the other side, got in his ride, and was on his way.

Yankee enjoyed his last minutes of anonymity, driving a red Ford pickup into history. Soon, he was going to be the most hated man in America or, at least, the devilish new character he created would be.

TWO

N aseem Amin knew all there was to know about Lake of the Ozarks. He knew it was originally Lake Benton, that it was about 130 feet deep, it had the most crowded docks, the most forgiving entries, and a few spots that were rather difficult to navigate. He spent the past month understanding his place in American history, just as he ran off to do whatever else his leader told him to. The lake became an obsession, and he became an expert. He didn't need to know all this detail, but it seemed important to know about where you're going to die. Unless he changed his mind rather quickly, Naseem Amin was there to die.

The phone vibrated and Naseem saw the message.

702-555-2312: IN PLACE?

He captained the big boat, but it seemed the boat had control of him. All of his certainty, all of the things he promised himself, all of them had become muddier than the Lake of the Ozarks water beneath him.

Naseem: IN PLACE. TEN MINUTES TOPS.
702-555-2312: PICTURES?

Naseem rolled his eyes and slowed the boat. He kept it steady with his left hand, gripped his iPhone with the other, and snapped a couple of shots of the boats in the distance. He took one of Ashlee and other lovelies on the boat, knowing that it would either offend this high man of Allah or turn him on. He was no longer sure. At this point, he barely even cared. He attached them to a new message and hit send. Was this some new form of terror porn?

Ashlee came up and put her hand on his arm. Naseem turned and looked at her and still didn't know what to think. Here was this beauty, with sun-streaked, sandy hair, high cheekbones, and piercing gray eyes, wearing a bikini that showed off her surgical enhancements, and she had unknowingly trusted Naseem with her life. She was dumb as a telephone pole, but, despite the mounting years and miles, there was a sweetness that completely caught Naseem off-guard.

"You good, baby? We doin' okay for you?" She kissed him sweetly on the neck, showing him a vulnerable side he had all but forgotten about in a woman.

She was wearing a red bikini with a scarf covering her shoulders. He lived eighteen years ogling this kind of titillating display and followed that with eleven years of loathing it. Now, after he thought he was totally protected from the West and its many mistresses, these past weeks had shown him he knew very little; all that was sure now seemed jumbled. Was this what God really wanted from him—to destroy people who did nothing but trust him?

"You're great," he said, and meant it. She tiptoed up and kissed him again, this time on the cheek, marking her territory. "Yay! I'm gonna go check on the others."

He reminded himself that these people flaunted everything he held dear. They raped the planet and made mockeries of their bodies and their lives. They were vermin and vermin needed to be exterminated. Where had that state of mind gone? Why could he not summon it?

"Okay. We're about ten minutes out. Get them up here."

She turned and mock-saluted him, winked, and headed in the other direction. He was eighteen again. For a moment, he almost felt giddy, a word he hadn't used to describe himself in years. *What an ass she had*, he thought as he watched her go. Where did all those years of training go? Was he really so weak that this girl could so easily turn his head? If one woman could so quickly undo him, what had he devoted his life to?

Naseem lived in America, just east of Hollywood in L.A., during his first eighteen years. His parents were devout Muslims but were as American as Ronald Reagan. They talked as much about the opportunities in America as they did of the Quran, and Naseem had really never considered any other life. He was an Americanized Muslim. He played video games, chased girls, and did not keep Halal. When he spoke about his experiences later, in London and other places, he knew what happened: he became one of *them*. He spat the last word like the vilest curse.

Then came 9/11, and everything crumbled. He felt the hatred and mistrust, not from his friends but from nameless people who did not know him and had no understanding of his family's commitment to this country.

One day, two ignorant, no-necked lowlifes harassed his mother just because of her skin color and the prayers she said. They were about to defile her, in a way that Naseem's father never could have understood, in her own home, no less, in some sort of drunken, hate-filled joke. Naseem had left for the store but turned around, praise Allah. He came back to retrieve his wallet and saw these men. He charged them with a strength he did not know he possessed, plowed straight into the one who was unzipping his pants and did so with such fury he sent the other man scrambling for the door. If they had stayed a minute longer, he surely would have killed them. He saved his mother that day, but, now looking back on it, he wasn't so sure he hadn't lost himself.

He felt shame, guilt, and anger—anger like no man should feel—and lost any sense of his place in this new world. He needed rules and guidance. He felt betrayed. His parents healed, dealt with "the situation," as they called it, and, most disappointing to him, adapted. This made it worse. He helped them move to a better neighborhood. Sad and bitter, they still bought this lie. They still were a part of America. He was now its enemy.

He moved to London, the home of the most radical of radicals. It took a while to completely transform from the American way of life, even when seen through the eyes of an increasingly radicalized Muslim, to the hard and rigid existence of his new world. But he hid his transition from these men who never knew the duality as it existed in America. He forced it down. He detached. He did not return or regret. He wrote his parents benign things so they wouldn't worry, but he was sure they knew what was happening. They wrote him of Muhammad's promises in the Quran. He read that book so differently than they did. His instructors programmed him with hate, stripped him of the individuality that America encouraged, and sent him further east, where he learned hand weapons in Afghanistan and bombs in Iraq.

He was given no fancy nickname. He was not broadcast across TV or canonized. But he was known and admired by the right people. The network used him in a series of four increasingly difficult kidnappings of minor Israeli dignitaries in the West Bank, and each job was done with precision and without emotion or error. He obliterated his old identity so completely that when American intelligence finally started picking up on him, they believed he was a British citizen named James Malhi. Unfortunately for the original James Malhi, a studious British nurse, that was exactly what Naseem wanted when he strangled him to death in his own London flat.

Now, a decade later, Naseem came back to the States to finish what Mohammed Atta and his other heroes began on 9/11.

Problem was he hadn't anticipated what the reintroduction into American life would be like. From the moment he landed, after more than a decade away, he noticed it all coming back. The smell of cotton candy, reminiscent of his high-fructose childhood. The sound of a video arcade. The flirtatious look of a young, pretty woman, whose face was uncovered, uplifted, and shown promise and verve. Little things he didn't hate. Things he hated to admit he liked.

And then there were the people. In the time since he came back, he sensed things had changed. Everyone was angry, but it was not just at him. It was at their government, at the banks, at everyone and everything. He was treated differently—better, like before.

He saw his parents, who were now old. His mother doted on him and shared her experiences with her American friends, who now looked like a rainbow of different colors and backgrounds. His father, in his absence, learned to watch baseball and halfway understood the rules, something Naseem never thought he would see. He sat down with him and filled in the details of suicide squeezes and hitting and running. A suicide bomber explaining suicide squeezes—the irony was not lost on him.

He knew he shouldn't have come. It introduced conflict. It

brought nuance. And nuance is the great enemy of the ideologue. At first, it was merely a niggling thought in the back of his head. But America was intoxicating. He took each job he was given and completed it, did it correctly and with painstaking detail. Now, it didn't feel the same. He was stalling. He was *thinking*. And now, on the day he had based his whole existence since his teenage years, his fleeting thoughts turned into full blown doubt. He asked himself repeatedly if this was how he was to spend the final moments of his life.

He still had two hours to decide before the explosion was scheduled. If he didn't take radical action, the beautiful Four Winds boat filled with beautiful women, on this beautiful day would be blown to the top of the sky. He moved the craft into place in Party Cove, one of the most notorious, debaucherous spots in the Midwest, one that stood for everything he hated in his previous life. All around him, under a brilliant sky, in a picture-perfect setting, he saw boats with half-naked and fully-naked women screaming, wooing, and taking shots at the behest of all the shirtless males around them. For a week now, he had brought in explosives that looked like rock concert speakers and dummy boats filled stem to stern with TNT. Once he started this, no one would be able to stop it.

All these attacks he planned and helped with, all over the Great Villain, and, now, at the moment that required his greatest singularity of mind, he couldn't summon it up. These people were dumb, crude, and most certainly without God. Did that mean they deserved to die? Ashlee and the other girls he hired in St. Louis to be his models for this trip were so naïve and so happy to be here. And now here he was, being their God.

The girls thought they were promoting a new movie. They were all in place on deck with T-shirt shooters and full of spirit.

They screamed and wooed. They were getting paid what seemed a pittance to him, but they were excited. Men would look at them. Women would be jealous. They would be paid and laid, as one of them said. That was all they wanted.

Naseem, fully shaved from head to toe, was now the most reluctant of martyrs with a head full of ideas and no concept of what to do with them.

He docked and tied on, went to the front of the boat, and kissed Ashlee. She beamed. She was enjoying being with a successful man, one with a little age on him. She was loyal and playful, and, after last night, when he could summon no more willpower, he could say she was some sort of fierce in the bedroom, doing things Muslim women couldn't conceive. She was not wife material, he thought, but now he felt almost certain he couldn't sign her death warrant.

He needed to think. He needed to not let his own mistakes obscure God's message. He had two hours to figure it out.

He told Ashlee he was going to take the jet ski for a couple of minutes. He would be back well in advance of their scheduled performance.

"Just have some drinks and chill," he winked. "And don't use up all the T-shirts at once."

Who was speaking these words? Who harbored this kind of feeling for infidels and vermin? The self-loathing Naseem remembered at 18 was back but for very different reasons.

"Okay babe." She looked at him, and his heart broke, not with love for her but with absolute hatred of himself.

He tore away from the boat, utterly unsure of what to do next.

THREE

Nathan Kinder worked all year on getting into Courtney Hollis' pants. He was relentless. It was something out of an 80s teen sex film, only, to this point, it was decidedly PG-rated.

The professors, students, and staff at the University of Arkansas-Little Rock agreed with Nathan on his choice of muse. She was a combination of innocent and pouty-lipped sexy, and she either knew she was the best thing alive, or she didn't, and both answers were equally as acceptable.

And now, he was about to make it. He had tried everything: cards, letters, flowers, poems, tweets, instagrams, and, finally, direct pleas for love and affection. Nothing worked, so he gave up, but that was the one thing she couldn't resist. She couldn't handle that he no longer wanted her, and he was talking to and possibly smashing other girls.

He didn't know she was a virgin. She didn't want anyone to

know she had never been that close with a boy. She played a role, and it worked until that damn Nathan had quit playing the pursuer.

She came to his room that day wearing a sundress that suggested everything. It clung to her curves and rode up her perfect derriere. She knocked on his door, gave him a kiss as soon as he opened it, and whispered closely in his ear she wasn't wearing any panties underneath it.

When their obituaries would be written the next day, no mention of their proximity was given to the press nor was there any hint of her lack of underwear. He was written up as a promising sophomore baseball star who hoped to one day coach, and she was called the apple of her daddy's eye in the *Fort Smith* paper's full-page spread. The men of Little Rock would have erected a statue to Nathan had they known where that afternoon was heading, but, in death, he was viewed as one more could-have-been.

* * * * *

Jackson Mingus, after ten years of teaching at community colleges all over Cleveland, finally landed a book deal. It was not as impressive as it sounded. He merely wrote a murder mystery—which Jackson, frankly, felt was cheating on his love of literary fiction—and published it with a small imprint of a large New York publisher, Pulp Town.

It was a good book, and he would speak at a couple of writer's conferences and hope that it got enough push to be able to write a second one. Today, he was off to meet with his college friend, Barb Detmer, who was a writer for the *New York Post* and in town covering the upcoming vice-presidential debate. Jackson proudly held a galley copy of the book for her, and he secretly hoped she could get it in the hands of someone on the *Post's* literary side. He figured it was unlikely she would know anyone, but she was the most famous person he could claim any connection with, so he figured it was worth a shot.

He walked downtown toward the Hilton and past a new restaurant they agreed on for lunch. He was just passing Crate and Barrel when the explosion came.

If Jackson had lived, if he hadn't been killed in the first wave of this most notable of terrorist attacks, his book had almost no chance of getting publicity. Jackson was paunchy, homely, and looked much sweatier than authors were supposed to. But in death, he was somehow transformed into a hero, all because he was in the wrong place at the wrong time. It was enough to turn that first novel into front-page news. Sadly, he did not live to enjoy it.

* * * * *

Two hours. That was all that separated Officer John Morales from his long weekend. He was going to grab his wife, and he was going to really surprise her. Through his side job doing security for a law firm, the one she always felt took too much time from them, he befriended a lawyer who gave him use of his house in the Hamptons for the weekend. Morales couldn't believe his luck. It was free house-sitting to the lawyer, but it was a godsend to him. He packed a bag for his wife, made up a boring cover story about meeting him near the train station, and he now stood a chance of pulling off the romantic fireworks she sadly said she never saw anymore.

He was in Times Square, on a midsummer Thursday afternoon, checking his watch every five minutes, waiting for the crew that was supposed to have been there half an hour ago. There was some fashion-related gala that was going to put a bunch of anorexic blondes in Lady Gaga outfits out in the middle of the square, shaking what little asses they possessed and generally embarrassing themselves. Morales had credentialed and overseen hundreds of these events—rock concerts and rallies, protests and politicos—but he hated the fashion events the most. The people never understood what was required in terms of permits, they all spoke in the third person, and, whether they spoke English or not, they never ever listened. He hated to lose his temper, but he always did when there was a fashion show.

He was checking on the trucks when the bomb ripped through them. It cut through the crowd with the concussion of plastic explosives and the metallic chink of the nails and glass that the bomb maker added. They skidded across the pavement and made the most hideous sound. Most people nearby never had a chance to even shield themselves and fell as the fireball made its way through them. They never heard the second wave hit behind them as the PA system and all the fashion trucks that Morales himself had waved into the park, filled with the same mix of C4 and foreign objects, cut down the large crowd behind them, rolling across the plaza like an army battalion, striking down everything in the way. Those who survived the fire looked down to see their bodies punctured again and again. They watched the blood slowly escaping through their wounds and heard themselves pay homage to their pain.

Morales survived just long enough to think about the surprise his wife would never know he so meticulously planned.

* * * * *

It was a summertime tradition to wait in line at the Shedd

Aquarium, always one of the hottest tickets in Chicago. In a city where summer meant long lines, the line at the Shedd was always the longest. Jeannie Gregg promised her kids she would stay this time. They tried this three times already that summer. Every time prior—due to the fighting between the two youngest, the heat, or the list of important things on her mind—she became too impatient to stick it out and would take the kids to another spot on the campus—the field, the planetarium, anywhere but that dreaded line.

But this time, she knew she couldn't disappoint them again. It was time to bring the Nook, the Kindle, the iPad, and think yoga thoughts while she waited.

She never liked the Shedd. To her, it was like paying to walk through a pet store. But her kids wanted to go, and she did love their love of ritual. To a professor of sociology, it was delightful to watch.

Almost twenty minutes had passed, and the line hadn't moved an inch. *Ugh.* Meanwhile, it grew longer behind her. She liked observing people, but she didn't like standing near them or with them. She would be a ball of nerves by the time she got to the front.

Jeannie hadn't noticed the man directly in front of her, carrying a simple college-style canvas backpack. She didn't know there were five others in line, two in front of them and three filling in behind. She didn't notice that the man's arms were shaved or that he was trembling slightly, as if he had a mild neural issue. She was too busy imagining herself in tree pose and keeping Hanna away from Kenny. She was too busy engaging in her own life to know that it was going to end—as soon as the force of hell emptied that backpack.

FOUR

When Caitlin woke up, a cowboy was snorting cocaine off her belly.

"Do you wake up from being passed out? Is that the correct terminology?" She looked down at the man, a low-budget Matthew McConaughey wearing a decent-looking western shirt with a ridiculous cowboy hat. White powder stood out like luminol in so many different places: on his nose, in his untrimmed mustache, on his cheek. He looked like a kid baking cookies.

No one else was around, but that wasn't a surprise. Cowboy certainly didn't want company. She had no idea who he was or where she was. All she remembered was a burning desire to get away from Britt, from whatever crazy shit seemed destined to go down. She knew she had traded one crazy for another but hell. That was the story of her life.

Work backwards, she thought. At times like these, start putting the pieces back together. She lay still, trying to take it all in. Her dress was pushed up just under her bra, but nothing appeared to be torn, burned, or bloody. Burgundy curtains were everywhere, brightened by nice track lighting. She was sitting on a comfortable and obviously expensive black leather couch. Okay, now she knew. She was at Oscar's in the back room. That told her several things—she knew people here, she would have to live this shit down, and nothing too horrible had likely happened. Her watch said one o'clock; she assumed that was p.m., which was bad.

To make matters worse, Cowboy was trying, rather ham-handedly, to take a selfie of him snorting cocaine off her belly. That was it. Her moment of self-examination was over. She snatched the phone from his hand and threw it against the wall like Roger Fucking Clemens. It made a loud scratching sound as it hit. The screen cracked, but it still glowed, daring her to try it again.

"What. The. Fuck." The cowboy said this like a commentator at a sporting event.

Caitlin smacked him on the side of the face and spilled all of the goodies on the floor while she got up and moved to the wall. The phone still worked. The dumbass didn't have a password, so she scrolled through, careful not to cut her finger on the newly jagged glass, and deleted the picture he snapped. She flipped through a few other shots to make sure he hadn't already taken some. She was pretty sure he hadn't. There were photos of Cirque Du Soleil taken from long distance and ones with a cowboy out to dinner with friends and with a beplumed Vegas showgirl. She gave him a little bit of credit—the photo of her as his buffet table was easily the most interesting picture he had taken in a while.

She sat on the chair across the room and continued to take stock. "I know this may be a major blow to your ego, but can you tell me who you are?"

The man looked taken aback. He ran his hand across his face

with his thumb like an eight-year-old with a cold. "Rick, baby. Don't you remember?"

"Have you violated me *in any way?*" She didn't think he had.

He looked sad and bewildered—like many of her dates, since her change of heart. "Violated?"

"Sorry. My bad. I don't know you. I don't remember anything. I don't think we have ever met. You appear to be snorting a Schedule Two substance off of my belly, and I don't remember shit about the last six hours. My guess is you or someone you know roofied me. I don't feel violated, but you might have a small penis. So I regrettably must ask again. Have you violated me in any way?"

"My penis …"

"Stop. I am utterly uninterested in your penis, unless it has unlawfully been inside any of my holes. You get one more shot or I scream rape."

"Shit. No. I ain't no pervert. I wasn't gonna start that party until you woke up."

She called bullshit on that entire remark and did a roll call of her body parts. Nothing seemed to be bleeding, stinging, sore, or chafed.

"Okay. How did we meet?" She was glad the guy had snorted the coke. His ego was going to need it.

"Paolo. He introduced us. You acted like …"

She put her head in her hands, and his voice trailed off.

He silently mourned the rail or two of coke spilled all over the floor.

In Vegas, if you were desperate enough, you could just snort the rugs.

Paolo was the night manager at Oscar's. He loved to introduce Caitlin to high-rollers. She came to understand, if not necessarily embrace, her occasional role in showing them around town. Her olive skin and jet black hair made her stand out even in the most enviable crowd. Caitlin possessed a lilting laugh and didn't carry herself like a mindless plaything. She didn't live in the gym, but she looked like she did, with long legs and perfectly crafted store-bought breasts to complete the picture.

She was stunning. And Paolo knew that once she started tying one on, she was utterly unequipped for stopping. It made for very happy customers, most of the time. Caitlin was the part of Vegas they would most remember—if they could remember at all. Paolo probably bought the shots and was keeping just close enough watch to make sure she wasn't getting raped. She hated him. But, she had to admit, he hadn't brought her at gunpoint. At least, she was pretty sure he hadn't.

Her head felt like hot asphalt. Her breath smelled like a fisherman's ass. What the hell happened?

The last thing she remembered was the official determination, made by her, that Britt was most likely a homicidal psychopath or sociopath. Caitlin couldn't remember the difference between the terms. She would have to look up the distinction later. But he was crazier than a monkey screwing a football, and she was pretty sure he was going to pull some major shit today. He made the mistake, as men often do, of thinking she was fifty percent more stupid than she was. Problem was he could still think she was brilliant and be wrong on that calculation. She put the pieces together over a period of weeks, and, finally, when he summoned her to his mansion in a lovey-dovey voice, she did not want to hear from him. She took smart girl lessons and didn't go.

She ran to Oscar's, which she was pretty sure he didn't know about, and let her hair down. Evidently, all the way down. She could boast armed guards and Mafiosi to protect her. What more could a girl want?

She checked and noticed that all he had done was pull up her dress. Panties were still in place. Shoes were close by. She found a mirror in the corner, wiped the marching powder that was still clinging to her nose, and headed for the door. "Nice to meet you. Clean up before you leave."

The cowboy looked crestfallen. She doubted he really thought he was going to make it with her, legally anyway. She opened the door and saw Paolo, Jenna, all of the Oscar's regulars and employees in the main room watching a single flat-screen TV. It told a story of devastation and showed bloody, wailing figures— not those from some distant, unpronounceable country but from America. Plumes of smoke, broken glass, fire, blood and tears streaming down the faces of mothers and children were all caught on film in that ultra-bright cinematic fashion Caitlin remembered from 9/11.

The announcers spoke in the voice they reserved for these occasions, as if they were simultaneously trying to read the news and take a poop. That voice meant bad news. This was easily the most significant attack on America since September 11, which happened many years before.

Caitlin stood stunned, trying to catch her breath as much as whatever drugs she took would allow. Despite their physical effects, she was sober now. If her meeting with the Cowboy hadn't done it, this certainly had.

She watched those images burn themselves into her mind and wrestled with a horrible, sinking feeling. She felt like she was going to faint. Caitlin was pretty effing sure her new boyfriend was behind the attack.

FIVE

Naseem gunned the jet ski. It was still early on during the extended holiday weekend everywhere but Party Cove, so he didn't have many other boats to contend with. He flew up the cove, the jet ski skittering over the calm Thursday waters, having become familiar with it over the past weeks, and tried to think.

He felt he found himself and lost himself in London. He found a purpose that was for a greater good, not just him and his needs. America was so untidy and so awesome. The positions he took in the radical schools where he went were much more understandable. They were saner. He understood who he was and what he needed to be.

But upon his return, freedom, American style, was a bigger rush than he expected, even though he lived it for years. Here people were not robots. Americans had eyes, mouths, hearts, souls, and genitals, and they used them all. What was he killing these people for? So he could be sent to the Promised Land? For seventy-two virgins? They might not add up to one Ashlee. And what about Ashlee and the others? Where was he sending them? For what crime was he willing to play their judge and executioner? Those were questions never answered in London. In London, there were no distractions and no realities. For someone brought up by people who loved the land despite its flaws, those questions were proving harder to take than he expected.

Two hours. He could tell the girls they needed to board another boat, make up some story about safety, and then give them some cash to get them to do it quickly. He could drive the boat to the least offensive spot on the lake, take the jet ski far away, and then call in a bomb threat to the police, so they could evacuate the area from all of the shrapnel and plastic explosives he had been planting for weeks. That would jeopardize his skin, but he was ready to do that anyway. At least, he thought he was.

He stopped the jet ski, killed the engine, and considered all of this. Sighing deeply, he prayed. The best prayer he could muster anymore. "Allah," he asked, "what do you want?"

As if on cue, he got a text. He pulled out the plastic bag and stared at the phone.

702-555-2312: ALL RIGHT THEN. LOOKS PERFECT. MOVING UP THE SCHEDULE. DON'T WANT ANY CHANGES OF HEART. I REALLY HOPE YOU ENJOY THOSE 72 VIRGINS. BET THEY'RE NOT AS GOOD AS THE ASS ON THAT BOAT.

Naseem stared at the phone. He didn't need to look up, but he did in time to see the explosion before he heard it. The boat raged out of the water, and all of the secondary explosives, put in strategic places he designed, went next. He heard the nails and other detritus whistling through the wind like the Grim Reaper's advance guard. Then he heard the screams—adults sounding like children and wounded dogs. Those sounds carried, vibrating across the surface of the lake. He let the noise tear into his brain for a second. He was the cause of this. It did not sound like triumph. Oh, to never be a failed martyr.

Naseem started his jet ski. He took out for the next cove. He knew what he needed to do. He just hoped he could avoid being seen doing it.

SIX

Pal Joey rolled everything big—big joints, big butts, and, mostly, a big entourage. Childhood friends, neighborhood pals, cousins, and half-brothers now shared in his success. His three albums and dozens of flows on other records skyrocketed him to one of the five or ten most famous rappers on the planet, and even getting to a gig was akin to moving a battalion across a river.

Hairdressers, make-up artists, logistics, sound, lighting—Pal Joey found a job for all his boys. And they all came along when he performed, even for a simple—and hella early—gig like the one today at one o'clock in the afternoon. *Who up at one p.m.?*

Joey adopted Lil' Wayne's six figure rule: don't go out or flow for less than six figures, and don't pass six figures up. So he was getting paid $100,000 for just showing up and flowing three songs—only THREE songs. He couldn't believe it. It was all to promote some movie called *Sabotage* which was using one of his tracks.

He was told the show needed to start at one p.m. sharp. All his people nodded when the promoters said this, but it signified nothing. They didn't say anything, but nobody told Pal Joey when the fuck to start, even if they were paying.

Five limos pulled up to Hollywood Boulevard, just up the block from Grauman's Chinese Theater. No doubt, many tourists, who would normally be boarding tour buses and putting their hands where Marilyn Monroe put hers, would be put out by all the commotion. But the thousands of people who came were a testimony to Joey's star power. His fans traveled. They made it out to see him that day, and what a day it was—a bright, high-sky LA day, the kind where sunglasses are necessary just to get out of the car, a beautiful day, like something out of a movie.

Joey wasn't in one of the five limos. That was too ordinary for this event. He was being flown in alone in a Sikorsky S-76 helicopter. It was giant, much bigger than needed, and fast as anything. Its wingspan was so big it required a clearing on Hollywood Boulevard which would normally be reserved for a head of state.

Joey got out of the helicopter, head down, and making the walk. He heard on TV about Elvis' thousand-yard walk before concerts and how it got him in the right state of mind. That's what he thought about as he walked down the boulevard through all of the fans. People who didn't even know who he was were still awed by the entrance. Both sides were barricaded off, and Joey practically bounced down the road. Man, he rolled with some swag.

The people who didn't know about the helicopter were on the other end, making their way to the front of the stage. It would soon be time. Already on stage was one of Pal Joey's up-and-coming acts, Manda, over-emoting her first single. She was trying to channel

Whitney and Aretha but sounded more like the cousin who did their nails. Still, it was just the kind of act Pal Joey wanted to add to his Straight Up Cash label. *The bitch could sing,* thought Joey, *and do other things as well.* Maybe the latter clouded his artistic opinion somewhat.

Three minutes. He was close to being on time. He was now backstage and exchanging handshakes with his boys. Joey would try to make it on time and do them proud. Maybe they'd give him a bonus or something. He was standing next to Raylon, his confidant, his best and oldest friend. Raylon's phone rang; he looked annoyed. Joey asked him what was wrong.

"Man, this the third time in twenty minutes. Damn promoter is blowin' up my shit."

"Yes," he told him again. They were ready. "Yes," he told them as soon as the song was over. He snapped his fingers and fidgeted. "Yes, Pal Joey will be on the stage in two minutes. Promise."

He closed the phone and threw it down. This mug was getting on his nerves. "Shit, man," he said to himself. He promised to do this, and he knew about the timeframe. "Let's get it on and get it gone."

But in the brief time that Raylon averted his eyes from his charge, Joey was half into a limo. There was a vision standing just outside the door. A blonde-headed, big-breasted vision with an ass the size of a horse farm. She was a Becky, slang for a white girl who loved black men and only black men. But oh, she was a fine-looking Becky. Raylon hated these distractions, because, most of the time, he was playing traffic cop instead of getting to enjoy the goods. He got paid very well so that Joey got to hit that shit, but that didn't make it any less fun to see your bro taking that all for himself. And she was *fine.* Raylon would have been tempted to sample that ass himself and ask for forgiveness later.

Joey was clearly introducing himself to this young lady.

"Yo, Joey." Raylon tugged at his shirt. "Come on. This shit can wait. She'll be here after you're done. Three songs. Where you at?"

'Yeah, I know," Joey said, turning to glance at Raylon with the slanted eyes of a serious dope smoker. The entire entourage smelled like a Thailand grow farm.

"We're supposed to be on now," he said, hoping to talk one more problem out of the way, knowing he was going to fail.

"I'll check witchoo in a few," he said. "Send the hype."

Big Brooza was his hype man. This was not what he was supposed to do, not at all. They were going to deviate from the plan so that Joey could get laid.

But hell, he thought. He'd be giving the audience more show. Joey would do his three. They certainly wouldn't complain about a longer show.

Brooza had seen this before. He admired Joey's new friend and nodded at Raylon with the look they gave when a classic piece of ass came Joey's way. Shit, Brooza was happy. He could plug his own release, out next week, on Straight Up Cash with plenty of guest appearances from his boy.

Raylon nodded and sent Brooza toward the stage. Roger that, thought Big Brooza. He was gonna rock this shit. Raylon pulled a walkie talkie from his pocket and asked the stage crew to go to Plan B.

"What's up, Callllllli?" Big Brooza hit the stage, plenty happy to fill the time.

"Y'all know me. From da SD. 619 baby comin' up da coast to fuck witchoo!"

The crowd, emerging from this rather impromptu setup, cheered wildly. Pal Joey was big and getting bigger. Brooza got his drops on the records, and most kids knew him. This was big stuff. Joey introduced himself to his new playmate, although he obviously needed no introduction. She looked upset and put off as he took her hand, and they got into Limo Number Four, a white stretch limo which had no current occupants, Joey's only requirement right now. The exterior was ho-hum, but the interior made up for it. It looked like a neon fairy cut an artery.

"Hi, Becky. I'm Joey."

"That ain't my name, boo." She put her hand on his neck and teased him. She didn't like being called a Becky, even though she clearly knew she was one.

"I know, but I ain't gonna rememba ya name anyway. Let's just keep it simple. You a fine lookin' Becky, but you a straight Becky."

The girl wanted to be offended and tried her best, but she couldn't be. This was one of the world's most famous rappers. This was her chance. All her friends and Facebook friends would soon know of her encounter. She snuggled closer to him, smelling his Versace cologne and the heavy scent of marijuana. Joey closed the limo door and moved to the back. Becky followed. She kissed him and undid the top button of his Coogi shirt. He kissed her back hard. Joey's pal Big Brooza made his case from outside the window, firing everyone up.

Then they heard it. A loud noise, like ten thousand concerts. It wasn't a gun. No gun sounded that big. It was a bomb or an earthquake. Then they heard a whistling, followed by more explosions. It sounded like fucking *Full Metal Jacket*. Two wheels of their limo tipped off the ground. Becky screamed. This limo was originally made for a presidential candidate and was perfect for a man who went straight from dealing drugs to selling records. He was as protected as a low-rent dignitary would be, and he needed the protection. He said that from day one. Half of 619 still remembered Pal Joey from when he was a civilian, a crack dealer. He could think of plenty of enemies. Was that what this was about? No, it couldn't be. This was way bigger than his sins.

The bulletproof limo sped off, not asking for directions, carrying only Joey and Becky. The driver locked the doors. If that bomb was meant for him, Joey should know better than to look out the window, but he just had to.

As they pulled out, he turned and cracked the window. He saw bodies. He saw blood. He saw his boy Sarge grabbing what looked like a stump for a leg and screaming like a girl. His best friend, mentor, partner-in-crime Raylon screamed from just outside his window.

"Please stop for me, please stop for me!"

Raylon didn't cry like that. This was bad. Their eyes connected for a moment and the pleading in Raylon's was unbearable.

The driver took that decision out of Joey's hands and sped up. Joey didn't complain. And that fact made Joey feel like a punk.

SEVEN

Caitlin forgot about her aches and pains. She quit trying to reconstruct her night. She now felt this destruction. She rolled these concerns around for weeks and strong suspicions for days. It just still seemed so dumb, though. Not dumb enough that she was still with him but just dumb enough not to call the police.

What would she have said? I've seen the maps that look like they're planning a military campaign? I hacked into his e-mail and saw messages that said some shit was going down on July 7 even though that shit appeared to be regarding a movie premiere? No, it was way too speculative to talk to anyone else. At least, she convinced herself of that.

The life had been sucked out of the room. Even Vegas, known for its decadence and its complete lack of connection to the rest of the world, was really composed of people from all over, and, at this moment, they might as well have been at home, looking at the screens and seeing their hometowns in flames.

The anchors were cutting between multiple locations—New York, Chicago, Atlanta, Miami, Missouri. There were reports that something just happened in LA. So far, nothing had happened in Vegas, at least that she could tell.

Well, if Britt were still here, that would make sense. She saw dozens of cities mentioned in that last e-mail, the one that scared her. If the e-mail was correct, there were more events to come.

Paolo saw her and seemed surprised. "I thought you left," he said, looking down at her and sizing her up, somehow simultaneously. "That's what I told your friend."

The unease intensified. "What friend?"

"The guido-looking guy."

Caitlin glared at him. That didn't exactly narrow it down in Vegas.

"You know. Your friend's boy. I saw you two at Bellagio a couple of weeks ago."

Shit, it was Tony, Britt's muscle. How did he know about Oscar's? How did he know about Paolo? She vaguely remembered seeing him that night.

She looked puzzled. "How did he know about this place?"

Paolo shrugged. "I gave him my card that night."

Of course, Caitlin didn't remember. She had been drinking and left all of her senses at the bottom of her third drink. This is why she shouldn't drink or do drugs—ever. She forgot things. She missed details. Sometimes she missed entire nights and their inevitable early mornings that followed. She always kept Oscar's as her safe haven and didn't let anyone know—until now.

"What did you tell him?" He could hear the note in her voice.

"I sent him on his way. I didn't like his look. I would have covered you either way. I suggested he check the high stakes rooms at the Wynn. He bit."

Oh, she was going to panic. She could feel it.

"I need a favor, Paolo."

He winked at her. "What you need?"

"I need a burner phone and a place to hide. And I need that little package I left in the back office."

Paolo didn't blink an eye.

"Follow me."

EIGHT

What were the chances he wouldn't be noticed? Here he was, a tall man of Arab descent, riding a jet ski like a bat out of hell while the sky rained smoke and ashes. Surely, someone would take note of that.

Lucky for him, he didn't have far to go, and no one rushing to the cove was thinking about terrorism. Party Cove owned such a bad reputation that everyone was heading there sure that some drunkard dropped a cigarette in the wrong spot and caused a diesel explosion. That explanation wouldn't last long, not with the size and once people figured out the shrapnel. But for now, it gave him just enough cover to round the corner, move sufficiently slowly through the no-wake zone, and take the jet-ski over by a community dock. It was early for most of the non-party cove visitors to have made it to the lake yet, so he was fairly safe in pulling in and eyeing his escape route.

Before he did, he thought of one problem that needed to be

taken care of. He no longer understood who he worked for, but he knew they assumed he was dead. That was an advantage he desperately wanted. He looked at the new iPhone, with its so many handy features he had come to love, and pressed the button to turn it off. If he kept it, he would be tempted to use it, and no good could come of that. He dutifully tossed it into the lake, saying a sad goodbye as it quickly drifted into the murk. He waited for a second to see if there were any chance it would float, but this was not going to happen. It was gone.

He had watched the lake for six weeks. In his mind, he was ready to die for the cause, but he didn't want to die without making it worth his while. Therefore, he had worked on finding an escape route should his mission need to be aborted.

If he was completely honest, he had provided himself with a relief valve. But he certainly hadn't considered this scenario—the cause he gave his life to would desert him.

Check that. The cause hadn't deserted him. That last text confirmed it. Yankee hadn't deserted the cause; he never was a part of it, just a clever and dedicated chameleon who duped them all.

The spot was between this dock and the marina, a large brown lake house with two levels, lots of railings and porch space. It was probably built in the 70s and was still well-cared for, but it was no longer prime space on the lake. As far as he could tell, save for one visit by a family about a month earlier, he had never seen anyone there.

On his last visit, ten days ago, Naseem did some reconnaissance. He left some real estate cards, things you'd see all around the lake, in specific places—on the back door and up on the car. He wanted to know if anyone had been there since his last visit.

He climbed from the deck and peered at the back door. The

card was still there. He discarded his life vest, practically jumped up the stairs, and went to the end of the deck, finding the jimmy he left there just in case. The back door was a screen door and no problem to enter. The house smelled musty and unused. Naseem searched for the owners' clothing and found them in the third bedroom. The man seemed to be tall and surprisingly thin, at least judging by his lake wardrobe. He sucked his belly in and put on a pair of flowery green shorts that were no match for the light-blue polo he found and was forced to wear. He hid his swimsuit above the dryer, went back outside, and threw the life jacket over the railing into the water. He didn't think any of it would be found for some time. He could not find any shoes that would fit him until finally, behind the door at the top of the stairs, he found a pair of flip flops that had obviously been discarded by a careless tourist.

In front of the house, there was a dark gold Buick under the awning, and, again, his cards were untouched. He used the jimmy and got the driver's side door open. The car looked to be from the early 90s and was easy enough to hot wire. The only question was would it turn over? Naseem tried—once, half a turn, disgusting sound. Again he tried, but got the same results, only fainter. He gave it one more time before he would have to figure out another plan. He waited. He prayed. The car sputtered for the longest time and then finally turned over.

He pulled out his wallet, the only thing he took with him. That left him with a thousand dollars in cash and two good IDs. He had no compass, but he could feel his way back to town. Now, he needed to get a new cell phone and warn his enemies.

NINE

Britt looked just dark enough to pass for about any ethnicity. White? Sure. Black? You could kind of see it. Mexican? Indian? Middle-Eastern? Absolutely. No one would mistake him for being Swedish or Scottish, but, for his purposes, it worked well.

He wasn't overly tall at about six feet. He was slender, well-built, and had his straight black hair cut long. When he went out on the town, it could honestly be said he looked like almost every other Las Vegas hipster with garish Robert Graham shirts and thousand-dollar jeans. He could have passed for thirty just as well as the forty-one he really was, and, even without his money and under ordinary circumstances, he could have bagged his share of Vegas beauties.

It wasn't the way he dressed or his workout-fit body that everyone remembered, it was his eyes. They were what first attracted Caitlin. They were so light you couldn't really call them blue, although that's what it said on his driver's license. Most people couldn't describe them, but they sure remembered them. They seemed to look right past you. For Britt, the flesh could be easy, or so he told himself, perhaps tired of being embarrassed by the end results. Women found him very attractive, and when they found out he didn't immediately fawn over them, they practically threw themselves at him. But then the object of his affection would open her mouth, and silly, stupid words would come tumbling out. She would call incessantly, and all of that dance floor attitude that initially attracted him would be gone, leaving only a needy and insecure exterior, regardless of how many inspirational quotes she might post on Facebook.

He liked Caitlin if for no other reason than she kept her mouth shut. He sought her out for her past, but he could see why his enemy chose her. He didn't always know what she was thinking, and, for Britt, that was rare. She was worth 100 of those VIP sluts. Her allure and what she represented meant, to his great chagrin, she was the only woman he could bring himself to be with; in other words, she was the only one who could help him perform sexually, a problem since his enemy stole his future. Beginning with his dethroning by the FBI and other agencies years before, his sex drive hadn't worked with any other woman in several years. For that reason, alone, he wanted her to stay by his side, join him on this strange, little journey he had committed to. It was a shame that now he would have to kill her.

Partly because of his performance issues, Britt's only interests for the last several years were money and intellectual superiority, most of the time in that order. He was sure that if he ever stooped so low as to allow himself to be psychologically profiled he would be categorized as a sociopath or worse, and, after today, you could profile him as a serial killer as well. But that was fine by him. Serial killers, although often too needy, were an amazing breed. They maintained the organizational capacity of a five-star general but, unfortunately, the emotional maturity of a needy four-year-old. He wasn't their kind of serial killer. He didn't need the recognition. He would make his mark, and then be quite happy to go away and never be heard from again.

The first few hours of his plan had gone swimmingly. If Caitlin had been a good girl and hadn't come up missing, everything would have been perfect. He admitted he once again underestimated her. He didn't realize she saw as much as she had, but he sent his best man—the best man still living, anyway—to handle her, the only living man that understood any part of his connection to this plot. Now that Naseem was charcoal in the middle of America, he couldn't think of anyone else who could tie him to the crimes that were already perpetrated and those that were yet to come. The smart dummies he sent with Tony didn't have a clue what he was about. They thought he was heartbroken over Caitlin running off with another man, and they would be paid too well to ask questions. They had no idea they were aiding and abetting the largest crime spree America had ever seen.

He needed one more piece of business to be concluded before he would definitely need to leave Vegas. He found this part regrettable, if only because he respected the cold-blooded planning of the Islamic terrorist group Sons of Allah and its leader Khalil Muhammad. But his plan was much more important, and, again, he stood intellectually superior to them and their silly superstitions. He could still be a fan and do his job.

The warehouse was on the outskirts of Vegas, well on the way to the desert. It housed various parts of the plan, all of them looking like normal business, known to very few other than Naseem and Britt just how deadly the plans were. The one ego trip

Britt allowed himself was the office on the second floor. It was overdone just for moments like this one, where he would have to meet someone who would expect opulence and would respect what went on to put it in an otherwise drab environment.

He rose to greet Muhammad, accompanied by two bodyguards. He had asked for this face-to-face meeting for years, but only the events of today proved his worthiness. He told these men years ago of his plan and then told them to come and celebrate the bringing down of the Great American Infidel. To Muhammad, he was one of them, a devoted believer. Britt cultivated this perception for half a decade with a seriousness that dovetailed through this entire operation. The link to Muhammad and all of the hidden killing machines over Europe and Asia was how he found Naseem, so brilliant, so tied to his cause. He died for a cause all right: Britt's.

"A salaam alaikum," Britt said as he rose. Muhammad grinned. The two had met via videoconferences and through other modern means, but, now, with America hurt and cowering, the sheik felt it more than fair to meet Yankee in person.

"Wa alaikum salaam," Muhammad replied. He sat down in Britt's brilliantly white office. It was quite large, filled with the trappings of manly success: the pictures of Muslim dignitaries Britt winced through and the large tank filled with exotic fish, which cost way too much for Britt's taste but seemed fitting for this place. It had been arranged today for maximum effect, just for this head of a terrorist state, with a chair for the great leader directly across from him, the whole scene feeling like a crucial moment in a gangster movie. In a way, it was. They were religious gangsters. Muhammad's two body guards flanked him, stared down by Britt's guards, who outnumbered them.

Britt needed to do it like an Old Testament usurper. If you're going to be the king, you've got to kill the king. No chance of defectors or angry righteous men coming back to give information about him. This man couldn't figure out he had been duped. Let him go to his god believing that.

"Great work, my friend," said Muhammad, who long dreamed of masterminding a major jihad on the United States. He scooted his chair closer to Britt.

"When you came to me with your idea, I thought there was no way you could get it done. Too ambitious." He thought about that for a second, caught in thought, gazing at the rings on his hands. "But you did everything you promised. I must admit, you have made an old man jealous but in the best way. You have been a great friend to me. I want to thank you."

"Give all the glory to Allah," said Britt, shaking his head, putting on his best act, the one that worked for all those years. "All Allah, your holiness. There is no god but God." This entire plan required him to know more about Islam than most mullahs. He made more trips than he ever wanted to the other side of the world. He detested most of the rank and file Muslims he met, though he detested most everyone, but there had been a few men whose presence stuck with him. This man was one. Too bad. Too bad.

"I have a gift for you, to celebrate our great triumph," said Britt.

Muhammad nodded his approval.

"More attacks are going on as we speak."

Britt handed him a large and expensively wrapped package. It was white linen wrapping paper with a gold bow around it. Muhammad opened the package, took care to work slowly through the wrapping, and laughed as he pulled out a gold-plated .45. He held the gun in his hands and turned it over. The weight surprised him.

"It has been many years," he said, laughing. The gift touched something childlike. "Am I Scaramanga?" Muhammad asked, remembering James Bond films from his youth.

"Ah, no." Britt said cheerfully. "No blasphemy intended. Just a rare specimen of a Palestinian gunmaker named al-Ibral. May I explain the significance?"

Muhammad's eyes blazed with delight. "Indeed." He handed the weapon to his friend.

"It's made for one purpose, perhaps not surprising," said Britt as he cradled the gun and lovingly stroked the barrel. He made a show of all of this, displaying both sides of the weapon, caressing it.

Muhammad chuckled.

"And what is that? Exchanging pleasantries?" He laughed at his own joke.

Britt smiled. The gun felt like a gold brick in his hand. "Certain and sudden death."

Britt stood and pointed the gun straight at Muhammad. He pulled the trigger as he aimed right between his eyes.

TEN

The driver was good. He took liberties, cut corners, honked as if he were carrying a wounded president, and made it from Hollywood Boulevard to the north 101 in record time. He was working his hands free phone to find out what was going on. He turned on the satellite radio to CNN and got the latest.

"Complete pandemonium ... attacks across the nation ..."

No mention of LA yet; that was too new. The talking heads were bringing on talking heads to analyze the situation before anyone had the slightest clue what was really going on.

He played this for his passengers as well.

In the back, Joey created some distance between himself and Becky, who clearly didn't know what to think. His worries that this had something to do with him personally subsided. But now, it was even worse. It looked like these people used him to draw a crowd. He heard tidbits from the radio about how shit went down in other places, but he was the only celebrity to be named in the radio broadcasts.

That seemed strange to him. He was a star, but he wasn't a household name by any stretch. Most teenagers would know him and every jewelry dealer in California already knew him but most white people and even older black people certainly didn't. Why would they choose him? Was it just some coincidence? He had to think more big names were coming. Certainly they wouldn't just tap little old him.

Joey remembered September 11. He remembered how the nation came to a standstill, how they honored the heroes, and took a couple of days to get together and mourn before returning to business as usual.

He thought this would be similar. But he was enraged they involved him. That wasn't his thing. He wasn't a Muslim; he wasn't anything really. He occasionally wore a cross, but that was as religious as he got. Why had they used him?

At this point, everyone seemed to think he was dead. One report from a guy so white he probably pissed milk said he was on stage in the middle of his set when this happened. Dumb fuckin reporters.

He had missed five calls from Raylon, but he hadn't even tried to answer any of them. He wasn't going to pick up the phone, at least not until he knew what he was going to do. This hurt him. He needed Raylon at a time like this, and he sure as hell knew Raylon needed him. But he didn't know what was up.

Was this targeted for him, or did he happen to be just another incidental casualty?

Becky picked up her phone and started to dial.

Joey grabbed the phone from her and turned it off.

"What you doin?"

"Sorry, baby. Give me a minute to think. They may have been after me."

"What does that mean?" Her attitude and swagger were completely gone.

All of that White Diesel he smoked a few minutes ago fucking left him in an instant. He had a plan. No bitch could control him.

Becky snatched at the phone, but Joey held it tight.

He kept his voice calm. "Baby. Stop. You may be in danger. I may be in danger. If you give me a headache, I'll just kick your ass out and my driver and I'll get my own damn self to safety."

Becky looked up at him. This shit was serious. She recognized he meant every word. She recoiled and sulked.

That was fine with Joey. He preferred silence at the moment. He buried his eyes with his hand.

Becky used his moment of inattention to steal her phone back.

Damn bitch wasn't gonna get away with that. He held his hand out and kept his gaze on her, until she finally gave him her phone.

Joey rolled down the privacy screen to speak to the driver, who just became his new best friend.

"Got any more info?"

"Nothing, boss. Just what you've heard on the radio."

"That's some bullshit. Drive north to the 405. How long should that take?"

"Fifteen, twenty minutes."

"That's it. Do that. And don't tell no one who you got."

"I turned off all our little devices. We rollin' silent."

Joey scratched his chin. "What yo name?"

"Marvin. Marvin Ellis."

"Marvin, I'm glad you my driver. You straight."

Marvin knew compliments didn't come often from this man.

He had driven for Joey's posse for two years and transported Joey himself on half a dozen different occasions. Yet the rapper had no idea who he was. Marvin was pretty sure this duty would stick. Marvin didn't mind too much. That was part of his job.

"Thanks. I'll let you know when I'm getting close." He put back up the privacy screen and looked for the HOV lane.

"Let me know. We fixin' to find a mothafucka."

ELEVEN

Grant Miller fielded a multitude of questions since the world started coming down around them all that day. What did it feel like being in the middle of something like this? They all knew the protocol, but, when it happened, was it different? What did he remember about it all?

After two solid years of being shunned, the attention felt good, but he answered their questions grudgingly. They hadn't wanted to talk to him much before this.

They were all supposed to be manning the phones and Internet, looking for leads, fielding the mind-numbing amount of unsolicited information that came into the FBI on a day like this. But they all wanted to know what it was like to be Grant Miller, the superstar who shone on September 11 and saved lives as a young agent, only to move higher and become a notable laughingstock. The questions he answered prior to that day had been mainly about the laughingstock part, so, if the situation hadn't been so tragic, he might not have minded this change in focus.

At one time, he was impressive physically—tall and thin with a southern frat boy haircut. His sandy brown hair was cut shorter now, and he was still good-looking, but anyone could tell he quit trying, at least for the time being. He gained twenty-five pounds over his peak shape, mostly around his waist. He didn't want to think of himself that way, but it got harder by the minute to ignore, and he finally faced reality and bought bigger pants. He found he didn't get noticed as often by women when he was out, and that cut both ways; it meant fewer questions about his past, but it also meant he was not the All-Star level closer he once was. In the moments when he let himself consider these things fully, he knew his drop in luck was more about confidence than his weight; he had lost his swagger.

That afternoon, when someone attacked Lake of the Ozarks—of all places—everyone assumed that St. Louis would be assigned to handle the investigation. It was, after all, the closest office geographically and generally considered better all-around than Kansas City. But KC drew the assignment, and Grant, now the king of all conspiracy theorists, thought it felt like one more shot at him. God, he hoped not, but he had reason to feel this way.

St. Louis, of course, was a conspiracy theory unto itself, when he was moved there to look into organized crime in the seedy east side of St. Louis, just over the river in Illinois. All the jokes that could be made about such a thing were made, and Grant endured it, ever-so-lucky to still have a job.

But those prying questions were gone now, replaced by the somewhat wistful questions of those who felt left out of the operation, desk jockeying while their rivals across the state were rushing to the lake to piece together what happened. Likely, many of the agents who weren't called immediately to help would blame him, as if he controlled everything but the weather. He knew he would just have to deal with it. Even in the worst case, in a day or two, some of the agents would be called to help. It would probably be mop-up duty, but, at least, they could brag to other offices they had been involved. Unfortunately, with today's well-lit map of tragedy, many offices were being called to duty.

He was at his desk, a cubicle under fluorescent light and a far cry from the corner office in midtown Manhattan he inhabited before the fall. His assignment was to try and put together a map of all locations the terrorists hit, between fielding calls from know-it-alls and crackpots. The whole thing didn't make sense. The attacks were all over the map, literally—east and west coast, north and south. More in cities, of course, but even a couple of attacks in the country. They did not have a fixed number of casualties, but they got the psyche right. Unlike past attacks, focusing as much on icons and people, these attacks happened anywhere. Hundreds were dead, and that number would surely rise.

The crazy callers blamed everyone from Islamic jihadists, to the Tea Party, and even one theory involved PBS. It was quite boring and demeaning, but it was all he had at the moment to do.

Grant heard a buzz in his earpiece. "Call for you. Line 7."

That was unusual. Line 7 was not one of the public lines. Almost all of his calls were routed from his direct line. But he was probably the most famous—infamous, really—employee of the entire federal agency, so some crank that followed his career might have figured out where to call.

"This is Agent Miller. How can I help you?"

The connection was good, but the caller was clearly driving. He could hear the background noise. Sounded like highway driving.

"Grant Miller? Agent Grant Miller?" He waited for an answer. Grant felt like he was playing a game of chess. He finally responded. "Yes, Grant Miller. How can I help you?"

"Okay, I'm pulling over. I'm on my way to see you."

"How can I help you?" More stern this time.

"Give me a number where I can reach you in ten minutes. Do this now. A cell line."

Grant thought about protesting, but there was something about this caller that felt completely different from the numskulls he spent the morning with. The man spoke with precision and purpose—and maybe a little fear. He broke protocol and gave him his work cell number.

"Thank you. I know that prefix. That is the correct prefix for your division."

Grant rolled his eyes. "I know that. Look, I'm not going to ask again. How can I help you?"

"In approximately seven minutes, your office will be destroyed by a bomb. I know, because I planted it. Please evacuate everyone, and I will call you after you are safely away. Do not tarry. You must leave at once."

Grant started to ask a question but could hear that that the phone disconnected.

He walked by Mandy, a once-junior officer who was now his boss, and stuck his head in her office.

"Bomb threat. Call it in. Sounds legit."

Mandy almost protested this direct demand from Grant, now her underling, but she saw his look and remembered who he used to be—an egotistical mess but one of the best agents she ever saw. She saw a hint of that in his eyes. She made the call and started the protocol. Grant was at the front of the line as they left the office.

Some of the people were griping as they filed past him out into

Kiener Plaza.

Grant tried to herd some of the people with him further away, afraid of the shrapnel reported in the other attacks. He used his badge and his voice to move people back, across the street, into the alleys, and away from the face of the building. "Get back! Get around the corner!" He waved and gestured as he moved himself.

He looked at his watch. Almost exactly two hours had passed since the original attack. He took a defensive position as his cell phone showed the clock turn to three.

Even braced and prepared, the blast rocked and surprised all of them. Then he heard the shrill whistle of the shrapnel and the urgent, bleating screams of those who didn't heed his warning.

TWELVE

D espite the similarity of their hometown's name, the seventh grade boys of West Memphis, Arkansas didn't regularly make it into the big city of Memphis, Tennessee. There was a river and much financially between them. Their lives were normally running the streets and seeing what they could make off of the largesse of the winners at the dog track. But today seemed different.

Today, they were coming to visit the Civil Rights Museum, and they were going to get to see the sights on Beale Street, which was more interesting on a Thursday afternoon than most places were on the brightest Saturday night. There were twelve of them, all promising students who hoped to one day rise out of their surroundings and make something of themselves. Seven were black, and five were white. All were poor. All were smart.

Jatrelle and Thomas were in front. They were talking about a certain girl back at school, tugging at their pockets, and wondering if she liked Thomas or if he was kidding himself. They were split on the answer to that question.

They would be lionized in the press as some of the youngest victims, their promise documented in several maudlin and lengthy *USA Today* articles. The articles were written by teary-eyed young Samantha Janitz, who dreamed of one day having children of her own. But how could you have children when this sort of thing could happen? Were you just sending your children into the world to be mowed down like Jatrelle and Thomas?

* * * * *

Gladys Diley puttered on her way to an Eastern Star event in Texarkana, Texas. The Eastern Star was the female version of the Masons. It had a lot less to do with secret cabals and a lot more to do with pot luck dinners and sewing circles.

She didn't like to drive her husband's pickup, but her car was in the shop. Needed alignment, he said. His old truck drove like it needed alignment, too. She laughed and thought it drove worse than her car did even when it needed work.

A week earlier, a man placed two boxes under the bridge up ahead. They were magnetically affixed to the structure. They were wholly unnoticed during their time there, by person or animal. Now, for a brief second, they started to whee loudly, before they exploded and ruined the watery tranquility of that spot. They caught Mrs. Diley just as she was overhead.

Friends remembered her as a loyal member of the Eastern Star and the Texarkana First Methodist Church. It would be several days before her death would be officially linked to the others.'

THIRTEEN

N aseem set his cruise control for 76 mph as he hit the interstate. He could call Miller back in a couple of minutes, after he knew the explosion was over. He hoped Miller listened to him. If he hadn't, he would be dead now.

Adrenaline had gotten him to this point. He didn't want to think about anything else. He had clearly been duped. If he needed clarity, the last text gave him that. Now, here he was, having failed in his effort to kill himself and to save the people he originally intended to kill.

What a mess. Was this what hell felt like? He felt sure of it. It certainly could not be worse.

He knew one thing for certain: if infamy loomed in his future, Yankee would have to live or die in it. He would have time to sort his own feelings, but he would bring it to that man who spit on everything he held holy and used him for his own gain. He spat on the prophet. He shat on Naseem.

The focus came back. The searing hatred lived as his brother for all those years, and the feeling that had been strangely diluted since he returned to this country ran back to him. Now, it focused on one man. Bring him down. Kill him or chain him, but make him pay for turning a martyr into a fool.

He wanted to drive 100 miles an hour, but, because of his skin color, he knew he shouldn't speed, not in the middle of Missouri where the people were predominantly white. Police could spot him across the way. Frankly, if Miller hadn't paid attention, he didn't know what he really headed toward anyway. He would find out soon enough.

He dialed the number Miller gave him. No answer. He took a deep breath and dialed again. After the third ring, he finally heard an answer.

"Miller."

"You listened."

"I did. I can tell real intel when I hear it."

They both paused for a second.

"The question is," Miller said, "why did I get it?"

"First things first. I have two requirements before I tell you anymore."

Miller said nothing.

"First," Naseem said, knowing the whole thing sounded silly, demanding concessions when he stood guilty of a thousand capital crimes. "First, you must convince the press that many agents died. You must not let them know that you were tipped off."

Miller was considering this. "I can agree. I will have to run it by my bosses, but I think we're okay there."

"The second concession is non-modifiable. It is not to be repeated to *anyone*. And it is nonnegotiable."

"All right. Let's hear it."

"I will not give you a whit of information without your express agreement."

"Time is wasting."

"When this matter is concluded, at the time of my choosing, you will kill me."

FOURTEEN

P aolo pulled his car around back, got perilously close to the back door, and then rolled down his window and whistled for Caitlin. She peered carefully out the door and then skittered into the backseat, staying low and pulling the door close behind her. Paolo hit the gas and turned onto the boulevard.

"What do you think all this means?" Caitlin really did not want to involve Paolo in all this, but it seemed clear that what masqueraded for logical thinking had certainly done her no good. She didn't trust him very much, but she guessed she trusted him a little, and that was more than she could say about anyone else at the place.

Paolo divided the world's problems into three categories: money, pussy, drugs. He calculated. "You into him for some money?"

"No, I think I chose a bad guy to hang with." She started to say more but thought better of it. "And I didn't stay sober long enough."

"You've been running with a rough crowd."

"Tell me about it." She thought about all she lost over the past year. It made her sick. She certainly didn't need a lecture from him. He turned on the radio. A new round of attacks began. No one had a solid estimate on total casualties yet, but it pushed 1,000. Attacks in eleven states. The radio announcers sounded like robots. No one knew what to make of this, least of all, Caitlin. She hunkered down in the back floorboards of Paolo's Mercedes.

"Where are we headed?"

"It's a little place over off of Rancho Santa Fe. My boy keeps it for moments like these."

Caitlin didn't recognize anything about it but didn't doubt it. There were hundreds of such houses in Vegas, where everyone is one deal away from needing a hideout.

"How long?"

"Fifteen."

She grabbed the Wal-Mart bag she had left in the back room, containing a change of clothes and some comfortable flats. It wasn't exactly high fashion, but she left it there just in case something weird happened, which happens a lot when you live your life blackout drunk. She checked to make sure Paolo couldn't get a free peak, but he had probably seen her bare ass a dozen times when she was hammered. She got everything off and back on and then slid down far enough to be out of sight, sitting in a weird yoga-like pose that hurt her back tremendously. She tried to turn on her side and worked on slowing her breathing.

Her smug assertion that Britt misjudged her now was replaced by the stone-cold observation she desperately miscalculated him. He was more than a low-level miscreant. It appeared she had been sleeping with the new Osama Bin Laden. Her back wasn't the only thing that hurt. It all hurt.

She questioned what she would need just to face tomorrow. She couldn't use her bank account, at least not at an ATM. She put some money away, but she felt sure he could trace that. If she made it until tomorrow, she could withdraw some, but it wouldn't take long to put that together. She would have to get her affairs in order, do whatever she needed to Paolo to make him let her borrow the car, and then hightail it for somewhere.

The hightailing it part she didn't mind. She wasn't cut out for this. She was a Midwestern girl. She still had a soul, no matter how many self-help efforts she made to remove it. Down deep, no matter how many nights she wound up with cowboys snorting coke off her torso, she really only wanted simplicity and the life taken from her. She wanted that back. At this moment, at least, she was not too proud to admit it.

Time crawled on all fours. Her back barked at her. She knew she couldn't look up, and that made the time seem all that much longer.

Finally, she could tell he was negotiating smaller streets. She figured they were getting close. "Here we are," said Paolo. She ventured a peek. He finally pulled them into a fairly new taupe-colored duplex in a block that featured nothing but. He pulled into the garage and then shut the door behind them. She started to head inside.

"Wait," he hissed. "Let me make sure it's OK."

He turned and nearly sprinted up the five stairs to the door. He peered in.

"All good."

She followed him in. Around the corner, she saw Tony, Britt's man. He dressed the part, black suit with a black tie. He could pass for a limo driver or maybe a thug. In this case, he was both. Tony pointed a revolver straight at her chest.

"Sorry," said Paolo, shrugging as she looked at him, aghast. "Just taking orders."

FIFTEEN

The gun recoiled in Britt's hand. Muhammad fell backwards, and the back of his head exploded. He barely bothered to look at the guards. He knew his men had the draw on them. They knew the plan. Britt heard four shots from each of the guards and saw the other men slump to the floor. Then, the guard on his left, on cue, turned and fired at the guard on his right, one less witness. Mission accomplished. Loose ends tied, almost all of them.

Britt had never shot someone at point blank range before this morning, not in his previous profession and not in this world of filth where he reigned as the king. He had plenty of people who did that for him. This morning's shootings had been in a more controlled environment and with a smaller gun. He marveled at the work this larger pistol did on a physical space. It sent blood everywhere. It caused him to breathe rapidly, much more rapidly than he had this morning, and, for a moment, he wondered if he would pass out. Good thing they weren't going to be staying there anymore. His ears rang from the blast. He was not cut out to be a wild west gunman; he knew that for sure. He hoped his last man didn't notice how rattled he was by all of this.

"Start the fire in here. We're done." Almost done, he thought. The text he received told him that Caitlin was on her way back into the fold. He calmly tossed the gun to Gianny, stepped around the blood puddles like avoiding a grenade, and headed for the backseat of the limo, where he could watch the results of his day. That had been the toughest part of scheduling the meeting with Muhammad in the first place. It must be done, but it sure put a damper on the victory party.

Britt fell for Caitlin, and that led him to believe she didn't know about his plans. He was glad she showed herself by reacting; otherwise, he planned on taking her with him as part of the spoils of battle, and he would have assumed that after the explosion that tore through his building, coupled with the mass chaos that was enveloping the nation, she would have never linked the events with her lover. Love, lust, or infatuation, whatever it was could turn even the hardest and smartest dumb and slow. He would file that away.

His limo impressed anyone who saw it, six screens tuned to the major news networks. He rarely watched them. Today, he wanted to see. They were filled with scenes of tragedy, tears and tumult, and with solemn-faced white people using their best worry-speak. No one knew what was next. No one dared to guess. Fire. Blood. Rubble. Tragedy. The disruptions were not massive in the sense of September 11, but the cumulative effect of so many, spread out over different geographical locations, felt much greater than other recent "tragedies." September 11 affected first-hand only those in the largest of cities. Britt, in the five years of meticulous planning for this attack, specifically chose all types of targets: cities, towns, and countryside. He chose ethnic groups and the whitest of the white bread. Some of the attacks had symbolic meaning to him; some were supposed to convey red herrings to those who would pursue; some were completely random just to add to that sense this was an overarching attack, but the plan itself was fully obscured.

Gianny came. He could smell the smoke from the fire his man set, which, along with the acid he poured on the bodies, would make positive identification a negative. Using the belt-and-suspenders approach, he would now add the final touch.

"Is this one 10 or 12?" he asked Gianny.

"12."

He dialed the number as they drove away and let it sit in the phone. As they pulled out, he waited until they were halfway down the block and then pushed send. Five seconds later, while he fully turned around to watch, the building took flight. It looked like it lifted from the ground. Gianny picked up the pace, knowing what came next: those whistling nails. He couldn't hear them in this instance, but he knew exactly what they did. He could see it all over the news.

"Let's go find my dear Caitlin and then head somewhere tropical." Britt said it as if he were planning a family vacation.

SIXTEEN

Grant made his way into the office building down the block, showed his badge, and barricaded himself in a conference room. He recoiled from what the man on the other line asked. Killing was a minuscule part of a federal agent's job. He was forced to do it once and sought counseling afterwards. Some hero he was. Most agents never had to kill. It was different than the tough-guy antics people saw on TV, but that mattered little. It just wasn't a major part of the job, and it certainly wasn't done on request.

"I didn't think that would be much of a problem," said Naseem, sensing Grant's hesitation. "If it is, I assure you that you will save many more lives. We can do this in the next thirty minutes or so."

"I will promise to abide by your stipulations," Grant said, feeling the bile settle in his stomach. Oh, how his superiors would crow if they heard him agree to this. He would worry about that later. "What do we need to do?"

"I've been listening to the radio, and I'm trying to piece all of this together. Many of the targets that were hit I knew about or planned. I know of some more that are planned for the next several hours. But some of the spots I was unaware of. I didn't know about Orlando or Nashville. This plan was bigger than what even I believed."

"What can we do now?" Grant put his head in his hands.

"I think the attacks will come on the hour. This is for psychological effect as much as anything."

"Is this a religious attack?"

"No. That's what I believed. That's what I signed up for. But this is all about him."

"Who's 'him'?"

"I doubt that I had his real name."

"What did he call himself?"

"He just called himself Yankee."

"Did he …"

"Let's talk attacks. We can profile him later."

Naseem was right.

"Write this down."

"I'm ready."

"He hasn't hit Charleston, South Carolina, and he hasn't hit Denver. In Charleston, the target is Fort Sumter. In Denver, it's the restaurant district just outside of Coors Field.

"Here's the tough part: the attacks need to seem like they've still gone on. I think you need to get major players—like network journalists—on Twitter to cooperate with you. You're going to have to pull people out of those areas, but let the explosions happen and have people talk about them."

"Why don't we want to show him we're stopping him?"

"Because he'll know something major's wrong."

"How do I know you're not just playing me?"

"You don't. But you're alive, so you've got that going for you."

Grant couldn't find a reply.

"I'm an hour away. We can meet wherever you want to, and I'll tell you what I know. I thought this was a holy war until a few hours ago. I was losing my taste for it then. But now, I don't know anything ..." He caught himself; he did know one thing, "except that I want Yankee, more than I want anything else in this world."

All of the words seemed hollow to Grant. An hour ago, this kook had been ready to die. The motive seemed very unimportant and lame to Grant at this point. He wanted to end the conversation. "I need to jump on this info. We've got half an hour until the next cycle. Call me ten minutes after that, and I'll see if I want to meet."

"You'll want to," Naseem said, now a forlorn and shaken prophet.

SEVENTEEN

Caitlin summed the situation up in a matter of seconds. Tony held the gun. She knew him through Britt. He was the real deal, not a garden-variety Vegas lightweight like Paolo. She stood far enough away that it wasn't an automatic kill shot like she was sure he hoped for. Professional killers like to control everything. Until she was square to him and closer, he would probably try to bluff her into thinking he would shoot. In fact, she knew he would shoot as soon as he got the chance.

She faced death or something seriously worse if she didn't take some action. She imagined stupid, greedy, horny Paolo was going to die too, though he was probably too numb and dumb to see it. Or maybe he would die, and she would go for a ride. She preferred death to that. She could play it safe, but that got her nowhere. It was time for psycho. Not much of a jump at this moment.

"You motherfucker," she screamed, like a coked-out demon, jumping hard on his instep with her high heel and smashing her large Coach purse against his head. She grabbed his head by the hair and started pulling, scraping, hitting, and kicking and put the bag in a position where she could grab her pepper spray.

Tony ran toward the pair, trying to break up the fight instead of shooting them both multiple times, probably what he should have done. Paolo didn't know what hit him, and he remained off-balance, trying to avoid bruising her. That would likely be Britt's job. She shoved his sorry ass toward Tony, and he lowered his gun. This unexpected move gave her a chance to get what she wanted. She gripped the spray in her hand. She turned to find the front door, not the garage door, and looked to see what stood between her and the door. She would have to make one corner, but that was it. She hit Tony with the bag, took a deep breath, closed her eyes, and sprayed those sonsofbitches with her pepper spray. She sprayed them and kept spraying until there was enough to subdue dozens of men. They coughed, yelped, and gasped as they both fell to their knees, or so it sounded. Then she turned and ran for the door. She slowed just before she hit it, grabbed for the lock, turned the deadbolt, and shut it behind her.

Caitlin opened her eyes and blew the air out of her mouth. She took off her heels and sprinted. She figured she had two minutes tops, maybe less. She could make the end of the block in thirty seconds, go deeper into the subdivision, and then try to find a house or something. She hit that corner and saw what she wanted to see. A young husband and wife were out in their yard, probably home for lunch.

"Help me! Help me!" She screamed.

This was Vegas. You could see their skepticism.

"Please let me inside. He's going to try it again."

Their eyes darted. This looked serious. The woman looked ten shades of wary, but the man took over. He grabbed her by the arm, and the three headed inside. He locked the door behind them.

"He ... tried ... to rape me ..." she said, tears from the spray pouring down her cheeks.

"Why didn't you ...?" the woman began, mad that her husband had brought some shoeless slut in off the street.

"He's a cop. I can't."

"What do you need?"

She took a deep breath. "All I need is for your wife to take me to Harrah's."

This seemed to mollify the woman somewhat.

"Please." She opened her bag to show that there were no weapons. "I'm going to be dead if I don't get out of here. I'll give you whatever you want."

"Let's all go," the husband said. His wife glared at him. He looked down the block again and then turned, resolute.

They went in their garage, put Caitlin in the floorboards, for the second time that day, and backed out of their driveway. Caitlin heard the wife loudly sighing all the way, but she didn't care at all. They were headed to Harrah's, and she was still alive.

EIGHTEEN

Naseem closed in on St. Louis, coming from the west and about to cross an antiquated bridge over the Missouri River. The sun sunk lower in the sky, mixing with the harmless clouds that lingered near the horizon. Because he headed downtown instead of heading away into the never-ending suburbs, he was making good time. He would be there shortly. He had traveled this route the other direction, on the way to what he had believed was his certain death. He had Ashlee and her friends with him. They rode in a rented limousine; all part of the cover he began to like. They bumped music by Lil Wayne, The Game, and the now-dead Pal Joey, another of his targets. These people were the antithesis of his religious training, of jihad. They liked different music, different than the muscle music he liked growing up in the US like Van Halen and Guns N' Roses. But their music was sometimes smart and alive and defiant in a way that his former life found treacherous and deceitful. He delivered those girls to their death. They were tried and convicted by him, and though he tried to save them at the very last minute, little good that did. They were too far gone, and he had been deceived by the greatest of deceivers.

Or was he? Maybe there was something in Naseem that wanted to take the anger in him and release it almost anywhere. Maybe he was an easy mark.

He expected to hear back from Grant but hadn't yet. He knew he would at some point, but, right now, Grant was probably still baiting the hook. Naseem understood this. He played this game on both sides: the fisherman and the fish. Right now, driving through middle America, he felt like the bait. He cringed every time a car passed him. He stood out in this land of white and black, not so conspicuous as he would have been twenty years earlier but still far from blending in. He was too dark to be Hispanic and too tall to be Indian. He was well-built, and that too added attention in this land of flabby and shabby. Ashlee called him the new exotic while running her hands along his smooth chest, swaying and bobbing to an MIA song. Ashlee, who because of listening to him, no longer existed and was blown in a thousand directions. She was one more soul on his soul. He winced and looked at the phone again, wanting not to remember.

As he did, the phone lit up. It was Grant.

"What took you so long?" he said gruffly.

"Just trying to clean up this mess you said you created." He hissed at the phone and then caught his breath and his temper and waited for any reaction from Naseem. He got none. "We got Denver evacuated just before it blew."

"You heard me. Charleston will be soon."

"I heard you. We've got people on it"

"I am in the Chesterfield valley. Where are you?"

"Okay, look, here's some ground rules. I am the agent. I am

willing to meet with you, but I call the shots, not you. I will get you out of the way of scrutiny for the time being, but this is my show."

Grant felt he needed to say all these things, although the pace of the last few hours did nothing but show that anyone having any information that would do what Grant did in Denver was clearly in the stronger position. Grant used his intel to call a well-positioned source in Boulder, who relayed to the non-ass-kissing agents in Denver. They weren't injury-free, but the death toll was much less than in any of the other attacks of the day. The police liaisons in each city were led to spin the story that authorities evacuated high-impact targets. Whether it would work was anyone's guess. Grant thought it was marginally better than not mentioning the attacks at all.

"Okay." Naseem said. The adrenaline that coursed through his veins and carried him over half the state evaporated. He needed to rest. "Tell me what to do."

"If you're in Chesterfield, go in the mall there. It's right off Highway 40. If you're coming east, you'll see it on your right. Exit 19. There's a massage place inside. Bottom floor. I'll meet you there in twenty minutes or half an hour. Tell the man there that you are meeting me, and he will put you in a back room."

Naseem didn't like it as a meeting place and thought about asking Grant how he knew this man, but he thought better of it. It would give him his first opportunity to begin cataloging his thoughts. If Grant turned out to no longer be the greatest of agents, he could always use that to his advantage as well.

NINETEEN

President Alexander Morgan had no idea what to do. There were not many times in his long and story-filled life this was the case. No one to name and blame, which was almost never true, and, apparently, there was no end in sight. Seventeen attacks, and the only lead whatsoever was from a disgraced agent more famous than some of his cabinet members. An agent supposedly getting tips from one of the terrorists sounded like the worst Trojan Horse scenario since, well, the first Trojan Horse.

It was dry throat, sweats, and heart pains—all-or-nothing—time. It was a Cuban Missile Crisis, a Pearl Harbor, a 9/11. The time never really came in his first seven years in office, and now it was the time that would define him.

There was no historical precedent for this and no presidential model he could turn to. Information changed the presidency more than anything else. It crippled Clinton. It befuddled Bush. Now, he had the first truly post-modern presidency in which the terrorist owned the same press opportunities as the president. Morgan was scheduled to speak to the nation in twenty minutes, and he had absolutely nothing to say. He bankrolled speechwriters who normally allowed him to say nothing very well, but, today, in his opinion, nothing seemed good enough.

The master of the political game, now toward the end of his second term, quit being quite so divisive, always his suit in trade. He wanted to strike a different tone in this situation in particular, being very careful now to craft a certain image for history to remember him by. He wanted to be bold and presidential and well aware of how these strikes, if they continued, would spur terror into the hearts of his people. The strikes were everywhere, and they were not limited to the coasts. They seemed, at this point, to be limitless, and they didn't seem to be a political statement, unless the statement was of coercing utter anarchy.

They were in the situation room, a sleek and modern room that was in direct opposition to the staid nature of most of the White House. The vice president had been shuffled off to parts unknown, and Morgan was left with his core staff, version 2.0. He still missed the grizzled veterans he put out of their misery after the first term. He wished they were here now. He really wished for their counsel.

"What do we do with Miller?" the press secretary, a handsome dolt named Steve Sanders, asked.

Dear God, who invited him? What a stupid question. The man was talking to the terrorists and was the only one to have a nibble. He was saving lives. The president knew every PR angle known to man and knew how to spin a story, but there was clearly nothing that they could "do with Miller." He would have to be watched closely, but, unless he unveiled a dynamite vest, they weren't about to do a damn thing.

"We don't have to do anything right now. He's supposed to make contact in a short time," he clipped his words dismissively, hoping this piss-ant would get the hint.

Sanders didn't. "You know how this is going to look if it gets out that he's the lead."

The president started to open his mouth, but Vanessa stepped in, like she always did.

"I really don't think you can worry about that right now, Steve," said Chief of Staff Vanessa Jones, who always said what the president wanted to say, only with less volume and fewer curse words. "He saved lives in those places. I don't know what you can do but trust it for now. Hundreds of people were saved."

"And we can't even tell people about it, tell them he was a hero again," said the president. "I think that's a bunch of bullshit."

"We need to keep this guy around. Maybe he'll talk to Miller. Even if it's a hoax, we can point to the lives that were saved."

Damn, time was short. Where was that speech? The president looked down at the computer in front of him and saw the latest carnage. He felt like he'd done nothing to stop it.

"Check your screens," said the press secretary, trying to rally. "Howell is sending over a draft." The aides looked at the screen. The president, who was not technologically gifted, was given an old-fashioned printed copy.

Jones got a call on her secure cell, and she stepped toward the hall to take it. The others pored over the words that the press room devised. It was trite, and the uneasy looks on the faces of those in the room gave the sense that no one liked the speech's direction.

The president was the last to finish. His face gave it away. He exploded, glaring at Sanders. "Fucking awful. Awful and hollow. There's nothing here! I've got to speak in fourteen minutes, and I'd be better off reading the ingredients off a cereal box. Tell them they have ten minutes to get me something better."

Jones was still on the phone as she came back in. She looked ashen. She finally cut the speaker off. "I'm with the president. I'll talk with him and get back to you." She shook her head and disconnected the call.

"We just got word," she said almost breathlessly. "Once the president announced that he was speaking, our new enemy announced they will be making a presentation at the same time."

"Who," the president glared, "is 'they'?"

"The terrorists, Mr. President."

The president said nothing. He threw his briefing papers high in the air and let them settle down over the room like confetti. He stood up and walked away, kicking his chair out from under him so it would surely fall behind him and topple loudly.

He was bound to speak. They had set a time. To change that time would appear weak and disorganized. But not one soul would be watching him when the enemy would be saying something at the same time. That sounded more interesting, even to him.

America's best option at this point appeared to be a man most famous for half-nude cell phone photos. God save us, he thought as he went to collect himself.

TWENTY

They were closing in on the 405. Joey would need to know fairly soon which way he wanted them to go. He wanted to have the driver pull off the freeway and stop, but he didn't want some jank-ass cop pulling up to see if he could help. Better to just keep heading even if they needed to turn around eventually.

Becky was sighing loudly, which only made Joey more determined to take his fucking time. This was some shit, and he was going to deal with it like a motherfucking monastery ninja from a kung fu movie. Let her sigh up all the oxygen on the planet. He focused.

"Look, I get you taken care of. But I'm protecting us both here."

Becky knew this was probably true, but she just didn't want to be happy about it. She looked like she was about ready to cry and talk a whole lot, so Joey held up a hand.

"I gots to call my boy. Give me a minute."

"I thought you said we couldn't use a phone."

"Not our normal ones. That shit's traceable. But I got it."

Joey remembered there was a drug phone in the limo. His people kept one phone in each limo for ordering whatever they needed: weed, hash, molly, yayo. That phone was bought at Costco or sumshit, and it wouldn't be traceable to him. He knew Raylon's cell phone number. It could be plugged into a thousand speed dials, and he would remember it from the street. He forever down with that boy. He didn't want to hear his boy's reaction, but he dialed the number anyway.

Raylon answered it on the first ring. "The fuck you doin' leavin' me?" Every word a question unto itself.

"Shit, man, I didn't make that call. Marlon my driver did." His name was Marvin. Raylon knew this, and Joey should have, too, as Marvin had worked for them for two years. But details didn't bother Joey.

Joey was careful not to say he was sorry even though he was sure Raylon knew that was half-bullshit. It's what he would have told Marlon, or Marvin or whatever his name was, to do in theory as well. It was just that reality was a lot scarier.

Joey needed to know one thing. "You sure you ain't told no one about me?"

"I'm straight. Aybody straight. Whole world thinks you dead."

"Let em think."

"What that chick think of dis?"

"She trippin, but she be aaaight."

Both of them eased on the street patois. When they spoke in private, they tended to get to the point.

"Who died?" Joey didn't want to ask this.

"Brooza, Manda, anybody near the stage. Probably twenty or

more. Blood was everywhere."

Joey just shook his head. He had lost friends, seen people killed, and killed one himself. That was part of the game, but this felt like it was on him. They were there because of his show. They were his fans and friends, his entire world, and they were dead because of knowing and loving him.

This shit was heavy.

"What the fuck is up?"

Raylon was just as blown away. "No idea."

"You got info on who booked this show?"

"Yeah, in the main e-mail. There's a computer in that car. Password is purple69. That promoter was blowin' up my phone."

"Yeah, I think he wanted me dead."

"Just like half of San Diego County, baby."

"This ain't about San Diego. I know that."

They sat there, two friends who knew enough to know that was true. They said nothing for a long time.

"You good?" Joey asked, knowing the answer.

"I'm straight. What you gonna do?"

"Gonna read me some e-mails. Then I'll decide. Call me on this phone if you need anything."

"Got it."

Joey rated two TVs, two motherfucking satellites, in the back. He turned one to CNN and one to MTV. CNN was all crying and bloody people. MTV was rocking Pal Joey on the screen, mean-mugging with Timbaland. The legend along the bottom of the screen indicated they were having a Pal Joey marathon. Hell yeah, he thought. There were some perks of this being dead shit— royalties.

TWENTY-ONE

N aseem did as Miller told him. He told the woman who seemed to be in charge that Grant Miller sent him, and she nodded. He went to a back room, which was about as private as a train station bathroom. On the wall was a large poster of the foot with Chinese characters pointing to the smallest regions, detailing their relation to the body as a whole. The room smelled like Asian spices, and everyone smiled and gestured at him.

People walked in and out, each time nodding or smiling and trying to get some recognition from him. He kept his head down. He didn't have a smartphone, which he had gotten used to in his time back in America, and he didn't want to see his handiwork anyway. The people, nice as they were, didn't know how dirty he felt. They asked him if he wanted "tay-bol massage." He didn't respond. He sat back and waited for Miller.

He wanted to drift off to sleep but instead spent his time remembering what he knew about Yankee. He thought of a dozen ways to protect his own skin, but, in the end, he reminded himself that six hours ago—had the plan gone the way he originally intended—he would already be dead. He needed to stay out long enough to take care of Yankee, and he needed help to do that. He had to trust someone, and, from what he knew, Miller was as good as anyone.

Muhammad, his leader, had been utterly convinced that Yankee was truly part of the cause. The man had been vetted and prepared, and the long process and numerous procedures made it unlikely that anyone could get through. But he clearly had. This seemed silly now. Naseem thought he saw it early on. Yankee didn't have the burn. At the time, Naseem could rationalize Yankee's icy resolve, a contrast to the ever-present, boiled-over passion he saw in most of his compatriots, as a positive trait. Now, it so clearly seemed hollow—because it was.

Naseem took the time and grabbed a notebook sitting on a shelf in the corner. He searched and found a pen behind a fake plant on a counter and started making notes: the places he knew hadn't been hit yet and rough diagrams showing where the bombs had been planted. There was still a part of him that hated to give up the information to the Americans, but he wanted Yankee more. He wanted him for a million different reasons, needed him dead, and wanted to join him.

It took several minutes for Miller to arrive. When he got there, he gave the woman some money, which was instantly pocketed. He was too far away for Naseem to hear, but he saw her point down the hall. Grant reached him and nodded but didn't shake his hand. He gestured for Naseem to follow him and then took him out through a back door to his car, which was parked in the fire lane just outside.

"Excuse me if I don't know quite how to handle this meeting," he said with little emotion in his voice.

"I understand."

"Thank you for alerting me to the explosion in St. Louis, but it's hard for me to say I owe my life to you," Grant said. He handcuffed Naseem's hands behind his back before starting the car. "I've got a place for us to meet. Let's go there and establish what the hell is going on."

Grant had gotten a room at the Hampton Inn under one of his personal credit cards that the FBI didn't monitor, just in case. He drove fast and ignored Naseem. The man probably hated the handcuffs, but he didn't know what other plans were in store. Grant had a look that no one would mistake for anything other than cop or serious thug. He wore sunglasses and looked used to wearing them.

Naseem was getting more nervous, which was not typical for him. He had to account for his actions. For ten years, he could have easily done so; now, it seemed like an insurmountable burden. He couldn't make the words that would justify this senselessness, the sense of betrayal. *Such is the curse of the human*, he thought. Give a man a true reason to die, and he will. Lie to him about that reason, and nothing seems like a greater offense.

Naseem had seen Miller in plenty of pictures. In those pictures, even at the end when Grant's life disintegrated, he looked poised and cocky, like he was in on a joke no one else got. Now, he looked older, much older. He was heavier and definitely very tired.

Miller's eyes darted everywhere in the car all the way to the hotel as if he were expecting another explosion. Naseem finally realized he probably was, given his reputation.

"There are no additional plans for you," Naseem said. "This is not a trap."

"I don't know what's going on. That sounds great. I have no idea. It could be a trap. No matter what you say."

The sun was tipping from day to evening, and the light took on an orange glow. Grant parked the car and walked around to the passenger side, making sure no one watched. He took the handcuffs off in one motion; most people wouldn't have known what he was doing even if they had been paying attention.

"I'm going to give you a little bit of slack," he said, looking into Naseem's eyes for the first time. "Don't make me regret it."

Naseem nodded and clapped him on the shoulder just in case they had an audience.

They walked in. No one was in their way.

The front desk lady smiled and nodded and offered both men a bottle of water. She seemed to recognize Miller. Grant smiled and accepted the bottle as he asked her if anyone was using the conference room. She checked a piece of paper and told them they would be fine in there.

Naseem realized Miller had brought people here before. He wondered whether the receptionist made the connection to the day's events and that he was responsible for the nightmares playing out before them.

They walked to the conference room, still sizing each other up. Miller surveyed the room. There were no hidden corners and no places to hide. He had been there before among the beige and navy colors and the utter sameness that set nothing apart from anything else. Here, Grant had sweated people they couldn't yet bring in but no one serious or deadly. Now, he saw the room with a new set of eyes, but no danger was here.

They sat down across from each other in heavy, uncomfortable chairs.

Naseem took his notes and spread them out in front of Miller.

"Here's what you need to know."

"Hold it. I'm in charge here."

"You keep telling me that." Naseem glared. He hated for infidels to scold him. Then he immediately softened. He had lost any authority for taking the high ground today.

"I'm going to ignore the tone of voice and remind you that you, in addition to your role in the largest terrorist plot in American history, also asked me for a rather large and unusual favor—one I'd say I don't have to comply with even if I'd really be happy to do it right here."

Grant drummed his fingers on the chair arm. "But I don't have to. I'll kneecap you, wait for backup, and then send you to St. Louis city jail and tell them not to kill ya. Tell 'em what you've done. Those boys downtown are criminals but they're sure as hell patriots. They'll do that shit for free."

Naseem knew Miller's type, knew he had to say that, but he also knew that it was true.

"I'm here to help," he offered. He knew how feeble it sounded. He gestured to his note pad.

This time, Grant let his attention follow.

"You've been a lot of help," said Grant, his voice teeming with sarcasm. "But show me what you've got."

Naseem rolled his eyes and continued with his train of thought. He had written the five places he knew for sure still had explosives: Omaha, Houston, San Antonio, Boston, Jacksonville. He had notes and diagrams and presented them to Grant.

"Why?"

"I thought I knew. I thought it was holy."

Grant took a deep breath and regained his composure. "If you ever visit a terrorist attack after it has happened, you will know there is nothing holy that could possibly come from it." He extended his help like a real olive branch. Grant needed his subject to cooperate, but they were wasting too much time. He needed to play nice, no matter how badly he wanted to do anything but.

"Why tell me now?"

Though he had anticipated it, the question caught Naseem off-guard. "I was duped. I was so sure I wanted to do this. Then I began to wonder. And then, just as I was ready to back out, he sent me a text saying the attacks would begin earlier than expected. It let me know he was not a true believer." Naseem spit these words out.

Miller rolled his eyes before he could stop himself. "So a Muslim killing Americans was okay, but someone else killing them wasn't?"

Naseem glared at him. He held his gaze an uncomfortably long time. "I am willing to put up with a certain amount of ridicule," he said, "but I have my limits."

Despite all of Miller's posturing, he had the weaker hand. Naseem had information. Miller could bluff all he wanted, but it was unlikely that anyone would allow him to truly harm Naseem. The terrorist was rallying and holding his own against this agent.

"Who is 'he'?" Grant asked.

"I know him as Yankee. That is the only name I was ever given."

"Did you meet him in person?"

"Twice."

"Okay, why did you trust him?"

"The right people in the jihad told me to. I wanted to die. I was told to die with him and for him."

Miller started to react and then thought better of it. This was the absolute best lead he and, as far as he knew, anyone had.

"Does he know you didn't die?"

"I don't think so. It was a lucky coincidence that I wasn't right in the middle of the blast."

"What do you want now?"

"I want Yankee dead. And then I want to die."

Miller wasn't going to belabor that point, but, despite his surface bluster, he wasn't sure he could carry it out. He'd have to give this a lot of thought.

"I've got some latitude. The boys from DC are probably going to come at some point, and they may not be as easy to get along with. If you'll come with me in my car, after a thorough search, we can eliminate the need for any formal arrest proceedings at this time. You can be lodged at our witness facility downtown and get debriefed."

Naseem wanted more, but he didn't press his luck.

"I want to be the one to bring him down," he finally said. "Personally."

"Well, I don't think that's going to happen, and, even if it does, it's not going to happen tonight. We need this other info as well. And that's all I'm really authorized to do."

Naseem thought about this. He had anticipated a more rogue operation, one where he had more control and could take a more direct route to his enemy, but he was realizing more each moment he was no longer in charge.

What Miller said made sense, and, frankly, it was just starting to hit him just how tired he was. It hadn't been his plan, but, at this point, he was fine with someone else taking the lead—as long as it led him to his target.

He nodded, just as Miller's cell phone rang.

Miller pulled it out of his pocket and looked very puzzled. He motioned to Naseem and indicated he needed to take the call.

It was a 702 number—Las Vegas. He had heard someone he

knew was in Vegas, someone he hadn't talked to in a long time. His stomach fell. Would she really call now?

He answered the call.

"Miller."

"Grant, this is Caitlin. I really need your help."

TWENTY-TWO

The message went up all over Twitter, Facebook, LinkedIn, and, most importantly, YouTube. It was loaded from a hundred different channels. "From the creators of the chaos!" was written cheekily on the screen, a far different tone from terrorist attacks of the past; this was done with enjoyment.

The message would be unleashed in one-half hour. On the web pages, an image of a time bomb counted down the minutes. The clock didn't move evenly. It stuttered, the seconds catching, stopping, and then flitting by like cards being shuffled. It gave the graphic a crazy feel as if not even the time could be trusted.

If everyone had not been in such a daze, it might almost have been funny: America waiting for a modern-day Dr. Evil. The public, awaiting his demands, seemed from a different era, a time when everyone watched the same networks and got the same information. But as it was, it felt like another allusion: Big Brother. Everyone was waiting to check in.

It infected everyone's Facebook feed, taking up more and more space, and refused to be ignored. Then people started sharing on Twitter, Tumblr, Instagram, and all the different ways people choose to connect. It came from a thousand different variations of the same theme: Sabotage, SabotageFriend, YouSabotage, Sa-Bot. Then the memes came. All the images associated with incessant and insipid quotes were modified: a smiling, friendly Jesus; Gene Wilder as Willy Wonka; a beautiful sunset. The types of backgrounds that carried friendly or funny messages passed back and forth. *Will you be there? Will you find out from your new leaders? Will you learn the meaning of Sabotage?*

All the memes, all the sites, directed the web traffic to one url: www.sabotage.com.

As promised, the clunky, unsettling clock image dissolved into a black background. The background stayed black for an uncomfortably long time—long enough to make this tense, uncomfortable moment seem that much more so. Finally, a grainy image flickered on the screen.

A man appeared. He had a mustache, oiled hair, and was wearing a 70s suit that would even make Burt Reynolds blush. He was outside in bright sunlight, affected slightly by the breeze. The colors were oversaturated like a bad send-up of old network TV. His message was faint, the volume turned down low. All of America leaned in toward the screen. They turned up their volume. They got closer and closer, trying to hear what this man said.

His words were platitudes, barely audible. He muttered something about "now is the time for all good men …" stuff you would test your typing skills with. America turned up the volume again.

"BAHAHAHAHAHAHAH!"

America collectively had a heart attack. The sound was

deafening, half banshee scream, half heart-stopping yell. The screen now filled with a bloody, evil clown, blood dripping down his chin, screaming loudly into the computer screens across the country. This type of video was not a new concept. It was called a screamer, and there were such videos on the Internet which were meant to lure you in with benign content and low volume and then would be turned up to the highest level. But in this case, given the mass hysteria that the day had already generated, it had just sent thousands of Americans into near-cardiac arrest. The clown wasted no time, having only one message, which he delivered in a shrill, high-pitched, and indelible voice like a Saturday morning show gone awry:

Hello friends, I am Sabotage. My message is mercenary. I want your money. Your politicians won't help, so I'll let you do it for me. Please make sure Kenner Industries is at thirty-five by 5 pm tomorrow, Tokyo time, on the Nikkei Exchange, or lots and lots of good people will die.

Then the screen went to a ragged American flag, then an old-time static pattern, and that was it.

People returned to their websites to find new images: clowns, other evil images, burning rubble. A window opened on many screens of a child crying, first a whimper and then a full-blown forlorn howl. There were new memes for a suddenly scarier times. They substituted the clown for Willy Wonka. The clown walked the beach like a seacomber. The clown now controlled their very lives it seemed. They delivered their simple message: double the stock price of a cruddy, out-dated stock, or more people would die.

TWENTY-THREE

Though Tony waited as long as possible to do it, he finally delivered the message to Britt: she had escaped. He expected hysterics, almost wanted them, but that was not what he got.

Britt took the news with equanimity. He realized he was probably still dazed from the killings he had carried out that day: first Seth and now Muhammad. He had come to the understanding, a little late in the game for his liking, that he could order cold-blooded hits without a problem. But pulling the trigger himself? He didn't know if he had the stomach to do it often. It was a funny thing to find out on this day, and it was clouding his judgment. All the killings, all because of him, were fine as long as they looked like a movie, something that someone else reported to him about, something he saw on the news. This morning with Seth was marginally okay; it was something about the way the body was positioned and that there was not much of a mess to deal with. He could probably shoot someone like that again. But pulling the trigger like he did in his office? He relived it all in his mind—hearing the report of the pistol, seeing a life explode, feeling the numbness and tingling in his hands after the blast, seeing Muhammad's guards riddled with bullets—and then he realized it was making him hard and without Caitlin! Maybe there was an upside here.

As soon as he had processed the good news, he now had to hear that Caitlin escaped? He didn't have a place to put that. His head was full. He needed a few minutes to conduct some of the most important parts of this entire masterwork, and his head was full of dying pansies and unfaithful women.

It once again reminded him that brains sometimes did beat brawn. She was worth more than any of his stupid men, even the best of them. He needed to find her. She was now the only real obstacle to pulling this off. The tough part was done. Much as he wanted to do otherwise, he would have one of the few goons he had left handle her. He wanted to see her face if he could, but that was secondary. She needed to be silenced. She had too many connections, including one which troubled him greatly.

For now, he was too blindsided. He had no rage for Tony. It was his own fault, really. He knew that. He needed Tony, at least for the time being, and wouldn't let any more emotion swallow him. Britt felt like this day, his masterstroke, was being swallowed up by his feelings. He thought he overcame having those.

"Do you know where she went?" he finally asked the thin voice on the other line.

"Not a clue, boss." Tony was cautious.

"She'll go somewhere big and non-descript. She'll wait there, and I'll bet she'll try to call Miller. She'll find out he's gone and then try to call common friends with the FBI and the like. She'll be worried about the airports shutting down. She won't go there."

"Where does she have cards?"

"I know she has one at the Wynn and the Bellagio. I don't think she'll go somewhere that nice. You know, the places where they know you. Try Treasure Island, or Bally's, or Harrah's."

"I don't have anyone at Bally's."

"Then start with the other two. She is the biggest threat left. Take her down, then head to Lake Tahoe."

"Will you be there?"

"No," Britt said. "Not tonight. I'm heading east. I'll meet up with you tomorrow night."

Britt wasn't going to meet up tomorrow night. The place was packed with explosives. Tony would be toast as soon as he keyed in the entry, like all of Britt's former houses.

Britt looked in the mirror. He looked ashen as he told his driver, "Take me to the airstrip."

He had an hour until the biggest fireworks yet. There would be no air traffic after that.

TWENTY-FOUR

The traffic on the Sabotage site was out of control. It surpassed Google and YouTube combined in the moments after the attack. A nation raised on *Die Hard* and thriller novels now saw their part to play—amateur detectives.

The site had the video that had scared the entire nation. It also had an embedded Twitter feed that scrolled its own results, #sabotage, with all of those who now worshipped it and hated it. These were mixed with the news reports of the dozens of people who were thrown into cardiac arrest by the crazy nature of the video. Within minutes, strange people made Sabotage tribute sites on Twitter and Blogger. These were receiving traffic, too. It was all too predictable in this era of digital sycophancy. Those who were appalled were much greater in number, but they didn't make websites. They just counted their children and locked their doors on this scariest of days. They were still numb to all that had happened but interested in what lay ahead.

The main Sabotage site was simple but eye-catching. The clown was featured, a baby wailed, and messages popped up and disappeared: *Your President Won't Help; You Stand in the Way; Do What Your Leaders Won't, and this Will Be Over*; and various other anti-motivational lines. Its main feature though was a box in the middle of the home page with a spot for a password.

As you scrolled over the box, the clown appeared and screamed at the user, "Guess the password! Get it right, save a life! Get it wrong, get a virus." The last words were said in the sing-song of a child, and the clown wrung his hands in mock sadness.

Within the next ten minutes, the virus counter in the bottom right hand of the page kept score. Initially, it counted dozens, then hundreds, then thousands of people, all sure they could crack the code and heedless of what their actions were doing. If they entered the wrong password, they were immediately forwarded to a new page where the clown danced and cavorted. It was funny and well-made but infuriating. While it downloaded, a virus infected the user's computer. It immediately began sending messages, first innocuous and then vile. Images of child pornography popped up on tens of thousands of computers which had previously been squeaky clean. The only way to stop them was to turn off the device. Some figured this out immediately, others were bombarded with truly depraved pictures of children and animals and things they would never forget. They filled their friends' e-mails with the same illicit filth. If their friends clicked one of those links contained within, they fell victim as well.

People had to disconnect to end the chaos. In a period of less than half an hour, the counter read 565,000. Those people were now off-line, but their passwords and personal information weren't.

The people who hadn't tried to be heroes saw a new image

emerge at the center of the Sabotage site. The clown walked to the middle of the screen and unfurled a sign that read,

NO WINNERS. ONLY LOSERS. AND THANKS FOR REMAINING TO WATCH THE NUMBERS SPIN. YOUR COMPUTER GOT IT WORSE. TRY AGAIN!

A new burst of code emerged. Within seconds, the computers that remained on the site now saw the power disappear from their units with a sickening groan that sounded like each computer was gasping for breath.

TWENTY-FIVE

Talk about protocol. Grant sat with a confessed mass-murdering terrorist, and the love of his life calls. Jesus, he couldn't not answer. He would be worthless talking to his subject, knowing she had just called. He hadn't spoken to her in two years, not since the aftermath of the incident, and he was shocked she would ever call him again. Did she need him with all this chaos? Was it that simple? He knew he had to answer.

He held a finger up to Naseem and walked to the other side of the room, careful not to let him out of his sight.

"Hi. What a surprise."

Despite the fact he wanted to talk to her more than anything, Grant knew he couldn't have a casual conversation with her.

Caitlin said nothing.

"Everything all right? I would love to talk, but you can imagine that we're busy."

"Grant, I'm so happy to talk to you. I was worried that you

were killed in the St. Louis attack." She knew its exact location and its proximity to him. "I feel so horrible. Now, I know for sure that I know who did it."

"What?"

"I know who is behind this, and he's chasing me now."

Grant looked back over at Naseem. Ice flowed into his body. How could this be? Was Naseem being straight with him?

"What makes you think that?"

"I got involved with a guy. He had lots of money and was kind of an asshole. My type of guy—right? I saw some documents I wasn't supposed to see."

"Like what?"

"A list. It included several of the places I know were hit, including the St. Louis FBI office. I should have called you right away, but I couldn't make myself think it was true."

"Who do you think this is?"

"His name is Britt Vasher. I'm sure it's not real, but that's what he goes by."

Grant was crushed and furious and mad at himself for realizing how madly in love he still was with her.

"Where are you?"

"I'm at one of the big casinos in Vegas. I prefer not to say which one until it's absolutely necessary."

"This isn't your number."

"This phone was given to me by a man who tried to set me up. I've memorized your numbers. This is the last call I'm going to make from it. I'm going to leave this phone here and let it get lost."

"Are you safe for an hour or two?"

"I think so."

"Okay, I've got one matter to piece together, and then I'll create a plan to get you out of there."

"Involve as few people as possible," she said, fear creeping into her voice.

"I will," he said, already half-annoyed she would choose to tell him this. What was her involvement?

"Grant?"

"Yeah?"

"I'm sorry for getting you into all of this."

Oh God, what did that mean?

He told her to get a new phone number and text him the number. Then he ended the call and walked slowly back to Naseem.

"Did Yankee have a girlfriend?"

Naseem nodded slowly. "That's why I called you."

TWENTY-SIX

In the end, President Morgan did speak at the same time Sabotage did. He had no other choice, really. The president can do many things but appearing to plan his schedule around terrorists is not one of them.

He stood in the White House press room, cameras snapping, and thought about how different it was than his other times in the room. Just as he was to begin, he decided to stop. He had always been an extremely talented gauge of how he needed to come across, and so he chose to make his remarks without a teleprompter.

"You know," he said, resting his elbow on the podium in a way he never did, "I've been in this room many times. I was here as a Congressional aide back in the seventies, and I was here as a Congressman in the eighties. I've been here and spoken to these same faces hundreds of times in the last few years. Most of the time, and certainly during my time as president, for every challenge that we have, every situation that needs to be fixed, there's still a joy and an energy that comes with being here. There's a sense of where we're going and what we're going through.

"But today, you know that some animals have torn at us in a way that we're not used to. They've hit us where we live, literally. As I stand here today, I am telling you that we are at the very beginning of getting to the bottom of this. Today is not a day of joy in this room. It is a day of resolve. This country has given everything to me. Its people are an endless source of pride and joy to me and to everyone who works in Washington, no matter what side of the political divide they may fall on. We may have bickered yesterday. Today, we hang together.

"I don't have answers for you right now. I only have the supreme confidence of someone who has seen this nation at work. We will put a swift end to this. We will restore this nation's safety. I ask everyone to report any suspicious activity and to join in whatever relief efforts you can. Now is the time to show these ..." he searched for the right, PG-rated word, "... vermin what we are made of. They will find out."

He thought about saying more and then thought of his days as a prosecutor. He had hit the right notes. Better to end a few words too soon than a few words too late.

He took a deep breath. "May God bless these United States of America. Thank you."

Jones stood to the side of the stage. She thought that was the best speech he had ever given. Off the cuff and nothing like the bland rhetoric that Sanders and his people had provided. It hit just the right note.

Jones met the President in the corner of the room. She turned and walked with him. "Best speech I've ever heard you give."

Morgan gave a laugh, straight from the gallows. "Yeah, too bad nobody saw it."

TWENTY-SEVEN

Traffic in Las Vegas was never a source of pleasure, but the normal traffic paired with the panic in the air from the word spreading about all the attacks plus a nasty rear-ender about ten cars ahead made it unbearable.

Britt tried to remain calm. He knew he should have hired a helicopter. He knew it, but he didn't want to file another flight plan, and he traveled the streets enough to believe that the time he allotted himself would be more than enough to make it into the air prior to his next move.

He wanted to get out and exact justice. He wanted to shoot the person who was so careless to not even notice that there was a car stopping in front of them in the face. He wanted to blow their brains out. He wanted to see it and do it himself.

But he knew he couldn't. He couldn't risk everything to satisfy his need for vengeance. The whole plan was still there. He was sure he would make it on time. He looked around for anything in the limo to calm him down. A drink? No, that was not going to help. He turned on the TV. He watched the flames and the crying. It wasn't perfect, but it helped. He was in control of that.

He calmed his mind. He wasn't going anywhere for a few minutes. He had time to reflect and nothing more important to do. He slowed his breathing and let his thoughts collect. After all, the most fun part about this entire endeavor was the thinking and the guessing. Will they or won't they? Will they stop trading on the stock? Will they inflate the price? He didn't think so. In fact, he hoped they wouldn't. Would others do the job for him? He rigged the entire situation so he couldn't lose whether the stock hit the target or not. He was going to rain the same hell down on everyone regardless of what they did. An interesting experiment in predicting what would happen in unpredictable situations.

You put the game in motion, and then you get to see how they respond. They went along with his model for the most part. Britt thought that the president might stand a little taller, talk a little more boisterously at the press conference, which he tried to listen to while simultaneously watching his own fun, but his Sabotage game made it difficult to respond—too much shock and awe, to use their phrase. He had them completely off-balance. He congratulated himself for that.

Britt placed bets in every direction, most of them with other people's money. He used bots to do most of it and hired hackers to place computer loops inside viruses. When you clicked on the Nigerian prince e-mail or the one promising nasty photos of your neighbor, you were giving him entrance to your computer. You created a stock account you didn't know existed. You were making him small amounts of money for months, and, now, you were about to make him a fortune.

Of course, Britt already had a fortune. He had more money

than he needed even if he never touched a bomb. But this was only partly about money. It was much more interesting than that.

Britt had money—lots of it. His father was the stately Connecticut patriarch who invented a new type of laser printer that made architects' jobs very easy. This was back in the eighties, when everything was bright and suburban, and his dad just let his alcoholic mother run the show at home while he made the money and screwed the help. Britt grew up with no grounding, no roots. He didn't want to be his worthless dad, and he certainly didn't want anything to do with his simpering mother. He was free to roam the neighborhood and do pretty much anything he wanted. So he came up with a plan. It was very simple, really. He wanted to be James Bond.

That's what he trained for. He was circumspect enough not to tell anyone, but every maneuver was calculated to become a spy: good grades, good looks, good choices. Spies needed to be spotless, and he was just that.

He made it into the FBI because he knew a friend of a friend. It was a first step, but they didn't see him as special. All the tools needed to become a player in today's law enforcement were not the skill set he planned for. Diplomacy, multi-cultural schmoozing, analytical ability—these were the coins of the realm now. Many agents never even fired a gun. The life Britt dreamed of no longer really existed.

So he was going to create it. Years ago, when he was still working within their rules, for the most part, he was halfway through a complicated but utterly harmless maneuver which would have made him a hero. That was when he was confronted by Grant Fucking Miller. Britt gave some information on bad CIA agents to deep cover men. It would raise his profile with the CIA and get him out of the FBI. They claimed it compromised deep cover. He doubted that seriously, but Miller confronted him. At that time, he was in the middle of his 9/11 poster boy power trip. He was an asshole, and he wasn't wise, or kind, or even reasonable with the knowledge he gained. He stuck it to Britt when he didn't have to do that. He ruined his career. Miller had it all wrong; he thought the bad guys were good. When he came in and started waving his gun around, that was how it had to be played. Britt and two of his confidants were cashiered out of the service; with the cover story, they resigned instead of face criminal prosecution. He secreted a letter in a safe from the deputy director of the CIA that acknowledged no official wrongdoing, but that didn't help. He would never be able to play again in spy ops. He was worthless as a clandestine, and everyone knew it.

For all of those years, being a spook was a fairly good replacement for having parents worth a shit, or real relationships, or any kind of balanced life at all. Grant Miller set him adrift and did so without an ounce of humility or any common sense. He didn't have any mercy or even take the time to hear him out. Britt knew he was technically guilty of what he was accused of, but these were not good guys. Grant never gave him the chance to show that.

Britt spent six months at the bottom of a bottle, figuring out just how much of his identity was wrapped up in his choice of career. He lost his edge with women, and he became painfully aware of how few friends he really had. Sometimes people find out these issues over time, one after the other. Britt was not so lucky. One day he was a fast-climbing spy with cover personas and an exciting, interesting life. The next day he found himself very rich and with his entire life gone. He needed a new purpose, or it would end badly.

Then it came to him: instead of being Bond, he would have to be a Bond villain. Over time, he came to see that as nearly as intriguing. No moral code to adhere to, and you still got the girl, if you wanted that and, he had to add, if you could get it up. You got more money, and the power was fucking off the charts. Britt began his plan to rid the world of Grant Miller. At first, it was that simple. Then, like any good businessman, he decided to expand his operations. He used his former connections and his looks to begin to carve out a plot. He enjoyed putting on the Muslims. That was fun for him, but he never forgot Miller.

When he found out that Caitlin moved to Vegas, he worked it into his plan to sleep with Grant's fiancée. *She was rather worth at least some of the trouble,* he thought. He imagined her running back to Grant about now. She would soon find out he was dead, as well.

TWENTY-EIGHT

O mega Flight 723 was an hour and a half into its journey, carrying 220 passengers between Las Vegas and Chicago. As they flew through the late afternoon summer haze, passengers were on their second cocktail, and flight attendants, having put away the snack carts, played on their phones. By the time they would land, it would be nearly dark.

Sitting in first class, Amanda Beezer was a redheaded goddess going to meet her new boyfriend in Chicago for a weekend to be spent exclusively between the sheets. She had her eyes closed and her thoughts clearly set to naughty. It was her first time in first class, and she could only afford it because the new boy paid. She tried to ignore William Mentzler, a Bermuda shorts-wearing retiree sitting next to her. He wanted desperately for her to talk to him and was being downright haughty since she did not reciprocate the feeling. He pulled out a John Grisham novel and pretended to read.

In the back of the plane, Rikki Vanover sat with her two small children, Jack and Grace, who were six and four. They were meeting Daddy in Chicago for a weekend at Wrigley Field and the Field Museum. The kids traveled often and were very well-behaved, and her neighbor, Naomi Felder, complimented her several times. "They are so much better than my children were!" she kept saying in a way that made Rikki truly wonder about how bad Ms. Felder's children had been.

They began the boarding process shortly after the first attacks, and the pilot had told them they were going to proceed since none of the attacks had involved aircraft. With all the new technology aboard planes, the tech-wired could keep tabs on all the activities and the wild theories that started circulating. In the process, at least one unlucky fellow would surely burn up his computer trying to guess Sabotage's password. They were watching the massacre in real time if they chose to.

Omega Flight 723 was chosen because those who were charged with putting the freight—where the airlines really made their money—on the plane had long ago become lax. For six months, a small electronics company from Las Vegas called American Securities sent packages on this flight every Thursday. They were always the same number and weight, and, for some reason, they always set off the bomb detector. For the first four months, the employees took the packages apart and meticulously inspected them. Time and again, they consulted with the company, who could not explain why they set the bomb detectors off.

"Our products have bombed, but not in that way," the jovial man at American always said when they would call.

Finally, they had seen enough. Despite the fact that the packages still set off the bomb detectors, the workers stopped caring. The packages were unopened by security each of the past eight Thursdays. Today, the same eight packages arrived, weighing the same and looking the same. They once again set off the bomb detectors. The men working in freight were used to this, and, frankly, were embarrassed they kept having to call the company every time. Once again and without even thinking about it, for the ninth straight week, they had loaded the packages on the plane.

This time, the packages were different, although it was still hard to tell. They contained C4 Plastique and a small detonator the size of a flash drive hidden in the middle of the package. It doesn't take a lot of explosives to take down a commercial jet, provided they are placed right. These packages, timed to detonate seconds apart, gave off a muffled bang at first, and then the main cabin sounded like an earthquake as the explosive met the reserve jet fuel. Parts of the plane fell away and the midsection exploded like an earth-bound meteorite. The lucky passengers never felt a thing. The unlucky ones had five or ten more seconds to wait. Then, for them, it was all over.

They made no screams and heard no explosions. They fell to the ground like ashen confetti.

TWENTY-NINE

They were so close to the airport. He could see it, but they were still slowed like something out of a madcap comedy, one stalled motorist, the rear-ender, and now construction. Britt had now had too much time to think. He was exhilarated and sickened by the two point-blank killings today. He analyzed them both like the Plays of the Week on SportsCenter. His hand was still numb from the recoil on the .45. His ears still rang. It was either the best thing or the worst he had ever done. It wasn't easy to tell which.

How long before they got on the plane? He was running out of time. He hadn't even heard if the plane had exploded. God, this whole experience was escaping from his control. He really didn't like that. Most importantly, had Tony found Caitlin?

He thought of her. The only woman who could fog the mind of the world's most important man. She was out there, betraying him, stripping him of his power. He wanted her, and he wanted her dead. She taunted him. She was ruining this perfect moment. Why had she left him? Didn't she understand? Did she still mourn that piece of shit Grant?

The pilot finally approached.

From the look on his face, Britt knew it wasn't good news.

"Sir, there's been a pretty significant in-air explosion. They're shutting all air traffic down until tomorrow morning."

Britt felt the life draining from his face. The bomb wasn't supposed to go off for another hour when they were close to meeting them in air. It was supposed to have a synchronized effect. Now, instead of being halfway across the country, he was going to be near the center of the crime.

Britt almost blurted out, "It's not supposed to go off yet," but he shoved it back in. He breathed so deeply it sounded like it hurt. He managed to nod and dismiss the pilot without shooting him in the face like he wanted.

"Well, guess I'm in Vegas," he told his driver, the only person around to talk to. "Take me to …"

Britt realized he had no great place to go. Time for a backup plan.

"Just drive," he said, gray from the news, "toward the city."

THIRTY

Now where could he do it? He had spots in his area, every agent did, but he was out of his turf. It needed to be slightly out of the way, but he was on a tight time schedule as it was. It didn't need to add to the confusion.

Then he thought of it: Highway 40 and Ballas—rich people driveways close to the highway. He would normally worry about people seeing, but, if it came to that, he would badge them and tell them it was national security. Today, no one would scoff at that.

He pulled off the road.

Naseem knew this stretch of St. Louis road well enough to know this wasn't normal.

"What are you doing?"

"Give me a minute."

Naseem didn't say anything, hoping this was something legit, but everything told him it wasn't. He had half-expected this, and, when Grant eased down a driveway, Naseem started getting out of the car. He got the door open and headed down the gravel road, but he slipped and came painfully down on his knee. He turned and saw that Miller was on him.

Grant spun him around and pinned him to the ground. Grant may have been less fit than his old pictures but was still powerful and strong.

"What …?"

Grant hit him across the face—hard. It wasn't enough to break bones, but it was enough. Then he took his knees and pinned Naseem's arm.

Naseem knew what he had to do, or he thought he did. Maybe Grant was fulfilling his duty. He sighed and let Grant put him in a choke hold. He knew this would be less fun for Grant if he didn't fight it.

"You killed my friends today. I can be as professional as I want to be, but you killed my friends."

Naseem looked up at him, a resigned gesture: do you want to talk?

Miller eased up. Naseem coughed, partly for effect, partly because he really hurt.

"Do that. I deserve it. Hold your rage. Kill me at the end! It will feel like the vindication you need."

Miller boiled. This man had just put him in a corner. He did not want agreement. He wanted this man to hurt like the criminal he was. But his last statement rang true. He had to agree with him, and he wanted to do anything but agree with him.

"You so much as sneeze wrong, and I won't kill you. I'll just put bullets in both your kneecaps and let the vermin do the rest. You won't get any virgins by my method."

"Why are you doing this?"

"Because I have to. Because I wouldn't be a man if I didn't.

Because you killed my friends."

"Welcome to my world. That happens to me every day."

Grant did not need this puke taking the moral high ground. He tried everything within himself to keep from doing it, but he kneed him in the balls—hard. Naseem sucked at the air and groaned, a sound Miller liked.

"Now I can be civil," he said, grinning at Naseem. "Get in the fucking car."

He roughly grabbed at Naseem and threw him back into his ride.

THIRTY-ONE

During his time as a politician, President Morgan had not always remained calm. He ranted. He raged. He sometimes said things that caused people to cry and caused him remorse later.

But today, almost as if his own speech had transformed him, he remained calm. This was his time of crisis. He was determined to handle this in a way history would remember.

He and Jones watched the Sabotage briefing alone. When it was done, and he overcame the sick feeling in his stomach, they allowed the rest of the staff in. Jones let him know about the Omega flight. He took the news with equanimity. Time for him to fully take control.

"What do we know about Kenner company? Are those assholes behind this?"

"We know next to nothing, about them, but there is nothing to indicate they are involved in this at all, sir. They're an old Utah manufacturing company. A few employees, some contracts of value. Worth ten, maybe twelve bucks at the most. Thirty-five dollars is out of this world. Their stock has been steady for years. They've always been fairly happy at their level. Make all their filings, not a single SEC complaint. A completely unobjectionable, minor American company."

"How's their stock now?"

"It's on a roller coaster. First ten minutes it plunged to five, and then it went up—a lot. Possibly connected to all the viruses that people downloaded. They may be being used to buy the stock."

"Or maybe people think they have to—their patriotic duty."

"That's what the website is trying to say. I don't know what anyone is thinking right now, but there haven't been any huge positions taken. It's all mom and pop stuff. They're scouring all the records right now."

The president shook his head. "What is his motive? Is it one person? Many?"

"I don't know. We don't see massive put orders, in other words, shorting the stock in great numbers. Any number more than 5,000 must be registered, and we don't have any put orders of that size on this truly unremarkable company."

"Well, it's remarkable now."

"What do we do? The director of the SEC wants to know if we want to pressure the Nikkei to halt trading."

"And make them look like the bad guys?"

"Say it was at our request."

"Well, what does that solve?"

"We have no idea."

The president scratched his chin. He took his time before responding.

"Don't negotiate with terrorists? That kind of thing?"

Vanessa nodded. "No-win territory."

"I don't know. What about people that have bought in the meantime? What do we do for them?"

"Wish I knew. Seems like their own problem"

"I don't know. I have run for years on the idea that I trust the markets. I may just have to put my money where my mouth is."

"Problem is, sir, it's not your money."

The president nodded. "Get me Grant Miller on the phone. I'm gonna either put that sonofabitch in chains, or I'm going to give him the keys to the kingdom."

THIRTY-TWO

Pal Joey had watched enough mob movies to fully understand the importance of revenge. Whether the Corleones, or Scarface, or the bigger drug dealers he had watched growing up, Joey realized the first rule of being a gangster was take care of your own. Now that no more shit had gone down in LA, he told the driver to head back downtown. He called Raylon and arranged a rendezvous point, where he intended to leave Becky and pick up his boy. He told the driver exactly where he wanted to go and then turned his attention back to his current companion.

Leaving Becky was a risk. If she said one thing to the wrong person, she would not only jeopardize the royalties Joey stood to gain from people thinking he was dead, but she might also put his life at risk, too. But shit was about to get real, and she didn't deserve to get caught in some firefight. Joey was going to learn what Raylon knew about the people who had hired him, and they were going to act on *something* and hurt *someone*. This was his moment.

"We gonna drop you off downtown," he said, no room in his voice for disagreement. "But you can't tell anyone what happened—no one, not even your best friend. It could put you and me in danger." Joey could think of no way that she would be in danger, but he figured it was good to keep her worried for herself if at all possible.

"I won't tell no one nothin,' baby. You give me your number so I can call you?"

"Give me your phone." He took her phone and dialed in his semi-private number. He hit send. It would be good to keep tabs on her, but he wasn't giving out his real number—only serious niggas got that shit.

"I ain't got this number on today on account of all this. Don't be callin' me right away."

Becky clearly thought her stock should have risen more than this, but she didn't say anything.

They practically crawled back downtown with all the traffic and met up with Raylon west of where the concert was on the residential side of Hollywood Boulevard. She started to get out before Raylon could get in, but Pal Joey stopped her.

"Don't talk about this until we can get it figured out."

"Okay, I told you so."

"You could get people in serious trouble."

"Look, I know. I just want to get home. I'm already hella late."

Joey frowned. He had serious reservations about letting her go. But it would be better than having her witness a murder if it came to that.

THIRTY-THREE

Grant put the car in gear and headed back to Highway 40. He knew Mandy would be nearly panicked by now. Doing what he did seemed stupid, one more boneheaded move that seemed ingrained in him. Naseem acted differently, as he would expect, but he couldn't worry about that now. He had played a hunch and a power profile, and he hoped he was right.

Mandy LaPierre, Grant's boss, answered on the first ring.

"Where have you been?"

"Talking to our source and getting more unsolicited information."

"Sources just come out of the woodwork for you, don't they?" The way she said this reminded Grant of all the pushback he had faced over the last two years. Almost all of the agents thought he should have been fired, and every day he dealt with passive-aggressive comments. He had no time for this.

"Do you want to hear it or not?"

"Oh, do enlighten me."

"I have received info from a second source indicating once again that Las Vegas has been the training ground."

God, please don't let her ask who. Please don't let her ask who.

"And who is this source?"

Why did he even ask? Of course she would ask that. He spit it out. "Caitlin. You remember her."

Mandy waited a minute before responding. "Grant, you fucking kill me. You can't be serious. How is your fucking ex involved in this?"

Grant's phone buzzed—call waiting. He looked down and couldn't believe his eyes. It was a day of reunions.

"Mandy, I've gotta go!"

"Bullshit you've gotta ..."

"Mandy, it's the president."

Not even Mandy had a response to that.

THIRTY-FOUR

Grant Miller was a very young FBI agent that Tuesday morning, September 11, 2001. He was late for work—a detail that would get left out of all press clippings, because they never figured it out—and was on his way from New Jersey, where he had found a place to stay in Fort Lee without being able to afford it, up to Midtown.

The story later was one of an instinct for the action; he stepped off the subway in the financial district, having heard the bombing of the first World Trade Center, but it turned out he actually needed a hat. His little cousin's birthday was the following Saturday, and he wanted to send him a Trade Center hat. He got off, knowing he was already late and probably going to get his ass chewed once again, and made it into the underground mall below the towers. As he stood in line for the checkout, he heard the blast, and, to be fair, he did some pretty great work.

Grant came above ground and carefully organized hundreds

of people in the mall, helping them quietly and quickly escape. He was in the plaza when he saw the second plane hit the towers and knew then what was going on. He organized, energized, and did whatever was needed, shooing hundreds of people away, flashing his badge, and making the sage call to keep from sending three rescue crews inside, where they would have certainly been killed if they were left to their own sacrificial instincts.

When the towers were disintegrating and the whole world seemed to collapse, Grant went against his own good judgment and ran back in one more time to grab a small Mexican woman who made it down most of the stairs but had no energy left. He saw she was confused; she didn't realize she made it, and she started to lay down on the stairs, away from all the people pushing past her. He put her in his arms, leapfrogged a falling construction worker in front of her, and ran like hell away from the hell that befell them. They made it to safety, and someone captured the image on video. And so, because of being late and ill-prepared for his little cousin's birthday, he began his new life as Grant Miller, hero.

The FBI, taking a pounding over security and their inability to talk with other agencies, was proud to have someone look good. They let him do Letterman and Leno, knowing they would have to pull him off any serious duty for a long while. That mattered little, because his bosses mainly considered him a lightweight anyway. He took a photo with President Bush that was used often by the White House in political ads; they were two mavericks with the same glint in their eye. Miller's goodwill and all-American charm could even help a president.

After his victory tour, he returned to the field office, and, being a name worth knowing, would occasionally get good tips. He uncovered a plot to kill a low-ranking justice department official, and, in 2006, he was given classified intel by a CIA operative that led to the arrest of three FBI agents who were giving serious information to organized criminals in Russia and the US, leading to the death of several CIA officials. Because of the way the information had come to Miller and his cavalier attitude throughout the whole endeavor, the attorney general could not bring criminal cases, but the rats were found and were swept out of the basement. Miller looked like a hero again.

With the FBI's permission, he wrote a lower-rung *New York Times* best seller. During the following several-year stretch, he became a well-known, slightly rich, insufferable asshole. He acted like a colossal dick.

Being on the cover of *Time* means people remember you. If you're with the FBI, you're not going to get into a lot of fights, like other famous people who don't have bodyguards often do. So during his platinum days, Grant was able to bring it with the ladies. With *your* lady if she was so inclined. He was young. He was good-looking. He was in FBI shape. Although he wasn't always "single," he was never married. He was an eligible and knowledgeable jackass of a bachelor. He taped enough sex to have started a porn site and was just smart enough to destroy the tapes before anything became public. He got comped at the Playboy Mansion—the FBI really wanted the press—and he swam at the private pools at the Bellagio. He lived it up.

Somewhere in his soul, he began to smell his own stink—not totally, but he got enough of a whiff to realize he had changed fairly dramatically and not for the better. And then he met Caitlin.

Caitlin liked Grant in spite of who he was. She managed the fame; she didn't dwell in it. She had been a party girl of monumental proportions before meeting him, an Army brat who had lived all over the world. She was not intimidated by Grant.

They met in Chicago, although she was from Kansas City. She

worked for a brokerage, not really engaged in her job, and she had no idea who he was when they met. This perturbed him. Most of the time he spent dealing with—and liking—"Aren't you …?" He was so angry he couldn't help telling her.

She still didn't know, and she thought his head would explode. When he finished with his soliloquy about his status, she turned up the corner of her mouth and said, "Well I like you anyway."

She played hard to get for months, and, finally, after she had sent a large dose of humility his way, she fell for him. For a while, their lives were like a movie montage. They held hands in romantic spots and made love passionately in the nicest places. He became kinder and less full of himself. He saw the difference in her, and *everyone* saw the difference in him. He realized how egotistical he had become when his assistant Mandy, now his boss, told him she was just days away from quitting before he had started to change. "I was willing to go work at a McDonald's if I didn't have to work for you," she said. It stuck with him.

He went on a presidential detail to the G8 Summit in Sea Island, Georgia. He had her come down right at the end, when the president had already gone. He commandeered a spot on Jekyll Island, found in the same quaint part of the world. It was early August, and all of the delegates had left the smaller island. It felt as if all of the islanders left them alone to run the place. She cooked dinner in their condo, and they took the top down on their convertible rental and drove around the entire length of the island listening to Broken Bells and taking in a sherbet-colored sunset that seemed to last hours. They listened to the sounds of the beach and marveled at the beauty of the ancient Spanish moss. Dragonflies swarmed them as they walked alone to the pier at the north end of the island. Caitlin mentioned that there was a wives' tale this was a great omen. He told her he believed that.

He half-expected a crowd to be enjoying a perfect evening like this, still summer weather, but they were nearly by themselves. They walked all the way out on the pier above the water. It swayed and danced beneath them as the sun finished sliding into the marsh. He pulled a ring from his pocket and dropped to his knee. He looked into her eyes and didn't say anything for a minute. She gasped and looked at the ring. Then he asked her to marry him. She said yes. She cried and fanned herself as the sun went all the way down, the timing perfect.

After an hour at the condo and Caitlin calling everyone she ever knew while Grant glowed watching her show such love and happiness, they walked out on the beach and found they were all alone again. They took off their clothes and swam, even though the tide was coming in. When they came out of the surf, they made love in a tide pool, holding each other tight and feeling the breeze whisper on their naked bodies. She joked about getting crabs, and he marveled at how lovely she was in the silver light. He told her to wait there.

He slipped on his sandy underwear and tiptoed back to the condo. It didn't matter; no one was around. He grabbed towels, blankets, and a bottle of red wine and went back to the beach. They found a spot near one of the gazebos, hidden not only from other people but from too much wind as well. They fell asleep so close to each other that it hurt his arm, but he wasn't going to move. He lay there for what seemed like hours, thinking about what mattered and what joy he found. He finally joined her in the night's final dream. The dawn woke them. She looked at her ring. He looked at her. Perfection.

It lasted all of three weeks.

THIRTY-FIVE

Britt sat in the back of the limo, listening to something sad and dreamy by Zero 7. He was on his second pass through Vegas. He was sure the chauffeur knew something was up. He could tell. Was he on their side?

Then he stopped himself. God, he was thinking so crazy. He felt several times that day like his faculties were leaving him. He had to make it through this and just hold on. He was drowning. He no longer felt like he was in control.

As he watched the familiar Vegas scenery pass again, he thought about where he had been for five years. He had wrapped his life around this plan, from his first illegal angle to being the biggest mass murderer in US history. He was thirty-two, the same age as Alexander the Great.

Alexander the Great was the pupil of none other than Aristotle, who was taught by Plato, who was taught by Socrates. It was hard to imagine a more impressive legacy. But Alexander, son of the great leader Philip of Macedon, took it much further. His domain was not academic. It was the entire fucking world. He fought Jews, Greeks, Turks, and even managed to subdue the greatest empire the world had ever known: Egypt. He conquered most of the known world. Alexander wept when he discovered there were no more worlds to conquer and then died. Was this Britt's fate?

He didn't know. His thinking was premature. He was not even out of the country yet. At this point, he no longer felt like Alexander. Now, after one short chain of events, he felt more like Nixon—at his most powerful and most paranoid—the man who had more second chances than any American politician. He needed to be back in charge. Earlier that day, he might have worried about how he would do without the adrenaline and the power, or what little remained of his adventure should he survive, or how would he survive success. Now, he hoped this latest setback would remind him he was far from done.

It was a tad surreal to see television screens lit up with his vision, his novel, his cinematic death score—majestic and electric and incredibly provocative. He wished Caitlin was here for more than one reason. Yes, for once he could use a woman, use an outlet for all of this power and desire he felt building in his body. And oh, she was talented at that. She also could appreciate his greatness, even if she couldn't fully understand it. That's what he hoped he had found in Caitlin. He knew she was Grant's woman and that was why he had initially desired her, but he also recognized just how rare she was. Now that he couldn't have her, he wanted her. Perhaps, she was the country remaining to be conquered.

It seemed strange that this entire endeavor might have been begun because of his sexual frustration. After all, it certainly wasn't started because of money. Ever since Grant took his real power from the FBI, he somehow seemed to strip Britt of his sexual power as well. Britt created elaborate stories to tell anyone about his embarrassing little problem, but he knew what the reason was: he was a eunuch now. Grant Miller made him a eunuch. He needed to get his power back. It was within his grasp today but slipping back. It reminded him of those elusive feelings for Caitlin, the ones that most closely seemed to border on normalcy.

The reason he could sleep with Caitlin was easy for any armchair psychologist to understand: she belonged to Grant Miller. Britt caused their breakup, engineered the incident that drove them apart forever, and made Grant look like a fool. Grant wanted Caitlin, loved her dearly, and Britt took her away. He could be a sexual stallion with Caitlin. Now, he felt sure that the power he wielded today, over Miller, over the president, over the nation, would be enough to bring him back. He was going to prove it tonight—one way or the other. He could almost believe it.

Tomorrow, he would know about the index and which endgame he would play. He would devise a new exit. Right now, with his extra time, he would see about life after Caitlin. He'd see what he could do with some new playmates. Given all of his power and all of the drama today, surely his dry spell was over.

He called his contact at the MGM Grand and placed his order. He finally had a place to tell his driver to drive to.

Thirty-Six

Grant picked up the phone and heard the familiar "Mr. Miller? Please hold for the president."

He had gotten several calls like this, most in the good old days when for whatever reason he became almost a confidant of President Bush, and still had the White House switchboard number in his phone. President Morgan, very politically different from President Bush, had still been a friend, and the two of them definitely made his continued career with the FBI a reality.

Of course, the calls stopped. Grant was political Chernobyl. They were no more able to carry on a friendship with him as with Osama Bin Laden. He was to be forgotten—until today.

"Miller? What the hell is going on?"

Thank God for the spared pleasantries. Morgan liked to cut to the chase.

"Mr. President, I don't know much more than you do. I'm just following the one lead that fell in my lap."

"And just how did that happen?"

"He's here with me if you want to ask him."

"Fuck you, Miller. I'm not talking to him."

"Okay then. I don't know. I am finding that at least some of this seems to deal with me as one of many targets."

"You know what some people think," Morgan said, trying to get at Miller, see if he could get him to respond differently than the president expected.

"I'm sure. There are a lot of people reconsidering their decision to let me stay on. You may be one of them."

"Did you have any involvement in this, Grant?"

Miller spoke emphatically. He knew this man, and he believed he could appeal to him. "Sir, I had no direct or indirect involvement in this. My only desire is to help my country and my agency in any way possible."

There was silence on the line. Miller knew he said what he needed to. He knew that the next person who spoke would be capitulating.

"I'm gonna direct that you get whatever support you need. God help me if I'm wrong."

"Sir, I have always appreciated your friendship and help. I won't let you down."

Miller looked down and saw his knuckle bleeding from his involvement with Naseem. He'd do a whole lot more than that if he had to.

THIRTY-SEVEN

Caitlin called in her one solid. Six months earlier, she had come upon a girl weeping miserably out in front of the Wynn and instead of passing her by—her default mode since breaking up with Grant—she sat down next to the girl. She had no idea why she did this. She asked what the matter was, and, upon hearing the girl's tale of being turned out as a trick by a boyfriend who deserted her, Caitlin let down her hard-as-nails guise ànd helped the girl. Tonya was of reasonable intelligence and very even-keeled, despite how Caitlin first met her. She soon found a job working in housekeeping at Harrah's, and she texted Caitlin just a few weeks ago to tell her she moved to floor supervisor. Caitlin came by and congratulated her. Now she returned, no texts and no calls. She left the phone given to her wedged into the seat of the cab and headed for the service entrance. She hoped the cabby's next ride took him to the other side of the strip. She was sure Britt would have some way of tracking it.

Caitlin asked for and found Tonya, who gave her a big hug.

She didn't waste time with pleasantries. "I'm in some big trouble," she said gravely.

Tonya looked surprised and then steady. "What do you need?"

"Is there a room I can have for a few hours until this all shakes out? One that nobody knows."

Tonya winked. "Follow me. That's easy."

They ran upstairs to the fifth floor—the one for the low rollers—and went to the end of the hall until coming to room 564. Tonya opened it with her master key.

"I'll say it's got a maintenance problem."

"Then won't the maintenance people come?"

"Don't worry, girl. I got this. You just get your head straight. Let me know if you need anything."

"Well, I do." She waited to see Tonya's look. It didn't change.

"Can you have someone get me a cheap phone from Wal-Mart?"

Tonya laughed. "Honey, after what you did for me, I'd do anything for you." She reached in the pocket of her smock. "Here. It's fully charged and ready to go. I'll get the charger from my car and bring it up too."

Caitlin looked at her. "But you …"

Tonya laughed. "The only people that try to reach me are bill collectors and booty calls. Long as you are okay with that, then you good. I'll get it later."

Caitlin shook her head. "Thank you."

"I still owe you, darling. You saved my life."

Caitlin watched her go and wondered if maybe she should have reached out to more people. This one had sure been worth it. After Grant, she just shut down. She had no friends, just strictly business. Now, when she couldn't get to her bank accounts, and all the money she made mattered very little, this was an excellent reminder of how important friends could be.

She texted Grant with the number and a simple "C." She was nervous and aggravated, and she grew quite surprised Grant hadn't called her back. She saw all of the times he tried to call her over the last two years. She ignored them all, amazed he was still trying. She assumed, at a time like this, he would jump to be her savior. But he acted almost bewildered. She wondered what she didn't know. She tried to calm down by reminding herself he was probably on a government plane by now if he was coming out here. Maybe that explained his silence. She hoped that was all.

But she wouldn't count on it. She trusted him once and look where it got her. She would wait, but she would plan as well.

She figured Britt had spies all over. How much he could contact them right now, she didn't know, but it was enough to make her want to get the hell out of the city. She had no idea how she was going to do that.

THIRTY-EIGHT

Mandy's look spoke of annoyance and disapproval. She texted Grant and told him to meet her at the Ritz in Clayton, a few miles from downtown. She then called her contact in Washington and did discover that the president happened to be calling her employee. She hadn't expected this. She knew Grant somehow stored up an amazing amount of goodwill during his years as an unofficial FBI ambassador from those who didn't actually have to work with him. She knew it saved his job. She didn't know it was enough to get a straight line to the leader of the free world. She would have to be more careful in how she played all of this. After all, that was how she leapfrogged him in the FBI hierarchy.

She sat near the door at the Ritz on an uncomfortable-looking leather couch at the edge of the lounge area. The room would normally be filled with a happy hour crowd at this time. However, this wasn't your ordinary day. There were a couple of older men wearing golfing outfits at the bar and a lonely lady waiting for someone to talk to her and sitting near the piano, which would normally have had someone playing old songs softly.

She stood as soon as Grant entered and walked over to him stiffly with a look of disdain and discomfort that made it look like she was walking in high heels for the very first time. Grant knew she thought he should have been fired for his transgressions, but he really couldn't figure out why she still disdained him so. After all, his mistakes directly led to her being put in the supervisor position she now had. They lost track of each other for a while, and then, after he was banished to the podunk Missouri outpost, she ended up there too. For her, it was less ignominy. She came from Missouri, and it was a step up, but it made it awkward for both of them.

He learned a lot over the last two years—what to let go of and that what Mandy thought of him really mattered very little. However, in this situation, how she processed the information would directly impact his ability to continue on the case.

He told Naseem to wait, handcuffed behind his back, in the car. Now, he second-guessed his impromptu meeting with Naseem, and he hoped he hadn't overplayed his hand. He didn't think Naseem would say anything. He hoped he was right. He motioned Mandy to follow him outside, where he could keep Naseem in his sights.

Mandy took a look at this man. His gaze was hard as he looked right at her. She tried to hold his eyes but finally looked away. She turned awkwardly to Grant and told him she secured a room off of the security entrance. She would meet both of them around the side of the building. Grant took Naseem out of the car, pulled on the handcuffs, and walked him around the corner.

"Be a good boy," were the only words he could think to say.

Naseem didn't respond.

Miller didn't know if this was good or bad. They walked into the small, dark room Mandy reserved for them.

"This is Naseem Amin." Grant made the introduction as matter-of-factly as possible.

Mandy nodded professionally and said nothing. She did not extend her hand. Naseem got the message.

She turned quickly to Grant, trying to keep control of this crazy situation. She decided she would ignore the presidential phone call unless he brought it up.

"How does all of this tie in to Caitlin?"

Grant shook his head. "I don't even know. This latest detail is news to me. I'm waiting on Mr. Amin to enlighten both of us."

Mandy turned to him. "Mr. Amin?"

Naseem's jaw clenched. He looked down at his lap for a moment and then spoke.

"Yankee never let me in on much of his overarching plan. I was in charge of three main items: logistics regarding planned targets, finding a shipping route that would allow us to get explosives into the distribution chain as we needed, and doing a little extra with the targets if I was given the impression they were more ... important."

"What were the important targets?"

"Los Angeles, New York, Chicago, St. Louis, and Lake of the Ozarks."

Mandy bit her lip. "Lake of the Fucking Ozarks. What the hell? The first three, absolutely. That would generate the most publicity. Why the last two?"

"To me, the last one seems to be the easiest and also the most closely related to what he wanted to do. Yankee said he wanted middle America to fear as well. That it wasn't just the big cities that we were going to hit. That made sense at the time, but now I realize it was to make sure that I was dead—put me on a floating pile of plastic explosives and boat fuel."

"But he knew you wanted to die. That was why you were there."

"Maybe he saw something in me that I didn't see myself. I left the boat to decide if I could do this to the others."

"I'm wondering if you left because you didn't know if you could do it to yourself."

She let the words hang. They served their desired effect.

"How did you survive?" She knew the answer but wanted to hear it from him.

"I was told that the attack was to be two hours later. He texted me, asked if I was in place, then asked me to send pictures. I did. I was having serious reservations by this point and took the jet ski out to decide what to do."

"Serious reservations," Mandy spat.

Naseem remained unfazed.

She had tried, but she couldn't break him, not in a million years.

He rallied. "St. Louis and Los Angeles were the only ones with specific targets. Yankee wanted to make sure that we got at least one big entertainment name. Pal Joey wasn't exactly household, but he was easy and comparatively cheap. In St. Louis, I was told to kill Grant Miller and was given all resources necessary to make it happen." Naseem looked at Grant.

Grant stared ahead. He knew this was a possibility since Caitlin called. But it struck him differently to hear it. He was involved in this but had no idea how.

"Why?"

"I was never told a specific reason why."

Grant interjected. "I assume it was because of Caitlin."

Both Naseem and Mandy stared at him. He wished he hadn't said anything.

"Why an hour later? Why not the first round?"

"Remember, the idea, at least what he told me, was to paralyze the country. Stagger the attacks. Keep people anticipating bad news. I assume he thought that all agents would be back in the office after the first attack. Give him enough time to get back from lunch and then take him out in Round Two."

Mandy's face remained stony. "Okay, I'll buy that. But why warn him? Don't you still hate America?"

"I hate you." He pointed at her "And I hate him," he glared at Miller but held his tongue about their run-in. "I hate your liberty and your privilege. I hate your race and your religion. But I don't hate you as much as I now hate him. All of a sudden, if Yankee wanted Grant dead, I wanted him alive."

THIRTY-NINE

The concierge at the MGM Grand did his job well. Britt tipped him a thousand dollars in cash and then gave him the man nod, the universal signal he would take it from here.

He was in the most opulent suite in the hotel with floor to ceiling windows and a full view of the man-made money pit that was the Vegas strip. He was there for half an hour, pouring a drink, watching his masterpiece, and mainly trying to take his mind off of the madness and think solely about the fun about to arrive.

Then they arrived. And oh, the man could score. There were four women, all absolute perfection.

Priscilla was a striking blond, tall with severe and short hair that made her look more distant and therefore more appealing. *Only a real man could bring her out of that shell,* Britt thought. She had surgically enhanced breasts that held up without a bra underneath her sheer shirt. She was his favorite.

Holly was tall but not like Priscilla. She had shiny black hair with bangs, not much in the way of breasts, but a shapely ass that begged to be spanked.

Jilly and Tilly were obviously related, a taboo that also spoke to Britt's heart. They were brunette and would turn heads anywhere they went.

Priscilla came over and kissed the nape of his neck, moving her lips up to let him feel her breath in his ear. She turned and kissed him and made a subtle move with her hand down to his groin. He could feel her hand there, but he might as well have been paralyzed. The feeling didn't arouse him. It didn't make him the least bit erect.

He thought of Caitlin. *Why wasn't she there?*

He thought of all the years Grant Fucking Miller cost him.

He thought about the terror and hilarity and triumph in his killings today.

He thought about the same things, and they all took his mind from these very beautiful women, taking him to a zone where no erection could, or would, or should ever occur.

He breathed like a sophomore girl about to have a panic attack and tried to pretend this was normal. He was a stud who saw it all and would have to be coaxed to even be attracted to them. He wondered if they bought it. He brought all four to sit with him on the bed. The ladies undressed and he helped. Holly's body, even without large breasts, was a wonder—smooth and perfect with a high, pert ass that any man would have killed for. Britt put on some Al Green—who couldn't get laid listening to Al Green—and Al hit his falsetto and urged them to call Al and come back home.

The ladies kissed and licked on each other in the forced way they did when they believed men wanted to see this. Jilly and Priscilla even seemed to like it.

Block it out. Block it out. Block out all this noise! Then he felt his cell phone go off. The only one he left on. He was relieved. He had a reasonable out. His breathing started to slow.

It was either Red, or Tony, or on the off chance Caitlin, but he knew instinctively it wasn't her. He pulled the phone out of his pants and saw it was Tony. This was either great news or very bad news.

"Ladies, I am sorry but I need to take this call," he said as if he were leaving a business meeting.

Priscilla, clearly the ringleader, said "Don't worry, baby. Go do your thing. We'll be doing ours. We'll be waiting for you to get back."

Hopefully Tony found her. His vision blurred. Maybe he had her already. Surely he did. Then he was sure he'd be able to pleasure his new friends. He was sure of it.

FORTY

The call from St. Louis came in to Vanessa Jones. She was still at her desk, alone in her room, just a few doors from the Oval Office. The office had all of the gravitas of the White House—large and important. It was where Haldeman helped Nixon dig his own grave, where parts of the Iran-Contra scandal were planned, and where the dirty work emanated. Jones didn't operate in that way. She saw her job as the president's bulldog, but she wasn't going to risk her own skin for anyone. To his credit, Alex Morgan never asked her to.

She picked up the cordless phone and walked to the window. It was important if they routed it to her at this time. She hit the green button and stretched. She felt tired and caged.

She could tell that Mandy LaPierre, her new best friend from the Midwest, did not like delivering the news. Chains of command be damned. Vanessa told her to call directly with any important information. Mandy's new orders were to ignore her superiors and report directly to her. Vanessa wanted to speak to whomever actually had any information, and she wanted it quickly to keep this investigation going.

"Well that was quick."

"Bad news travels fast."

"What's up?" Jones had the ability to sound like the friend you were having coffee with. It endeared her to secretaries and heads of state alike. She never lost her common touch.

"Well, ma'am, it looks like Grant Miller's girlfriend was a confidante of our prime suspect."

This information made its way onto Vanessa's iPhone a few minutes earlier, right after the president spoke with Grant. This was shocking and beyond anything she wanted to tell the president. She had to consider if it had bigger ramifications than just this matter. Had the FBI been harboring a traitor, or had Grant's protestations of innocence, half-hearted as they were, been true? She decided she would wait a while before giving him this news.

"I heard that a few minutes ago. What does it mean? Confidante? Is that what they call it now? Sounds more like concubine to me."

"This information comes from Mr. Miller and from his informant. I don't have hard corroboration outside of the interrogation room."

"I don't need corroboration at this point. I need information. I need to know ahead of time, so I can keep the president from going down a blind alley. Have you met Mr. Amin?" Mr. Amin sounded strange to say.

Mandy paused, having considered this herself. "I met him. He seems … credible. Maybe too much so. Maybe he's just saying what we want to hear. At times, he seems angry and truly interested in seeing Yankee—that's his name for him—brought down.

Sometimes it seems like he catches himself trying to save his own skin. Maybe this is natural. Maybe he's just playing all angles, just like everyone else."

"What's your hunch?"

"What else do we have to go on? I left him every opportunity to abandon his story, and he didn't. He really does seem to have saved some lives."

"I've been saying the exact same thing. What do you think the next step is?"

"Straight up?"

"Always." Vanessa Jones wanted nothing else. She viewed her current job as a prelude to much larger perches. She wanted her boss' job after a little more seasoning. She was not going to be burned by making bad decisions on such fundamental matters. She liked Mandy LaPierre from her brief dealings with her. She wanted to hear exactly what she was thinking.

"This is absolutely unorthodox and if I could think of any other plan in the world, I would gladly give it to you. My boss probably doesn't want me to suggest it."

"Do tell," Vanessa commanded. She had a strong idea of what would be said.

"I think Grant and Amin should go to Las Vegas, where Caitlin is. I think I should accompany them along with guards. I just checked with Washington. To this point, they are still the most promising sources we have."

"What if Mr. Amin blows up the plane or does something similarly spectacular?"

"Well, Ms. Jones, that's why I volunteered to go. I figured it was the best way to show my belief in this plan."

Vanessa let an inch of mirth creep in to her voice. "It does do that. What is the objective in Las Vegas?"

"He hasn't hit Vegas yet. It's an obvious target. It means one of two things: he's there, and that's why he hasn't hit it, or he's going to hit it and hit it big. Either way, it makes sense for us to be there, to rendezvous with Mr. Miller's friend, and then to see if it brings us any closer to our target."

This was big and risky. Putting a terrorist on a plane was the kind of thing that could make or break a career, not just Mandy's, but Vanessa's, too. As unassailable as it seemed to be, one slip up here and she could find herself out of a job.

"That's the best you've got?"

Mandy swallowed. "I think so. Miller is a touchstone even if he's not involved. And for the record, I don't think he is. I think it was either some payback from his little exploits with the princess, or he was just an easy target symbolizing American extravagance."

Jones nodded. That was her feeling and the president's as well. They were at this for hours and had not one single other credible lead. They had to take some risks, or this day was going to get a whole lot longer.

She let a little prayer slip silently from her lips and then asked, "Where do you want me to send the plane?"

FORTY-ONE

G ive him weeks, Tony thought, and he could find about anybody in Las Vegas. He knew bartenders, strippers, bookies, and hotel clerks. He knew craps dealers and high-class hookers. He knew how to triangulate people. If you had enough time, it really wasn't a problem. If you had only a few hours, it was.

Trying to find someone—someone who was hiding—in a few hours in a city of this size was impossible and unthinkable. It just wasn't going to happen. He couldn't believe Paolo. First, he tipped her off that Tony was around and then he brought her unsecured—really? It was unbelievable. Paolo was soft. He didn't do this kind of work often. He couldn't go down that road too far, however, or he would have to admit who put him in that position: good old Tony. So when it came down to it, Caitlin's continued ability to breathe was really his rather large mistake. Easy or not, his best bet was just to keep moving and looking and hoping Britt wasn't going to have *him* killed.

He should have taken the shot in the condo, but his orders were to catch her, not to kill her. A very stupid decision on Britt's part. He wanted to remind Britt of this, that you eliminate a target when you can but thought better of it. The rage and the brow beatings were all part of what you put up with to deal with psycho assholes like Britt. He wouldn't be with him always; he knew that. Regardless of what he decided to do with the rest of his days, he would just as soon stay employed right now, if he could get these thoughts about Britt out of his head. And he certainly wanted to stay alive. Both of those sounded good.

The whole situation made it necessary for him to kill Paolo. He hadn't enjoyed this. He liked it when the people he killed were considerably "badder" and not just a soft moron from a club. The dumbass should have had her hands tied, or handcuffed, or something when he brought her in—fucking amateur. It was a mistake that cost Paolo his life.

Tony had told Britt everything. Britt had this bloodless quality about himself. He would look as sanguine as an old-hand spy handler, and then, when it served him, unleash all of his emotion at once. He kept quiet when Tony told him the story. Then he, cold as an iceberg, simply told him to find her, find her wherever she was.

That was two hours ago. Even though Tony made a dozen phone calls and visited two properties himself, he knew it was no use. It would take jackpot luck to allow him to find her anytime soon, anytime when it might actually mean something.

He looked at his watch for the dozenth time. It was time to be a man. He called Britt's number.

"Found her?" Britt cut right to the chase.

"No luck. I'll probably need a lot more time. This is a big city, and she's a smart girl."

Silence. Tony hated silence. And Britt knew this.

"I could …"

He had no idea what he was starting to say. How he hated silence.

"I …"

Again nothing. Britt was letting him twist.

Finally, Britt spoke in that icy voice that was far scarier than any emotion he showed. "That's a big miss, my friend."

Jesus, these guys never knew what they were asking. "I know. I'm gonna keep looking."

Emotion crept back into Britt's voice. This was ruining his scenario. This dumb bitch and her intuition was going to cost him everything. "Fuck it, Tony. You didn't get the job done when you had the chance. I'm going to put someone else on Vegas, someone she doesn't know. Your next role is in Tahoe. Go to the cabin there and thank your lucky stars you're still employed. I'll call you first thing in the morning."

Tony nodded and then realized he hadn't spoken. "Okay, boss. I'll talk to you in the morning. Sorry, boss."

"Look," Britt said. "Clean up these things. Get to Tahoe. I'll speak to you in the morning."

He spoke to Tony as if he were a seventh grader.

Tony was near the strip, so he headed out of town toward the interstate. He had eight hours ahead of him. Tony checked the gas. He had enough to get him out of town but would have to fill up once and maybe into a second tank. Might as well do it now. He was sick with the conversation. He liked it a lot better when Britt screamed.

At the gas station just outside of town, Tony pulled out the credit card Britt gave him and charged the gas. He leaned against the Escalade and twisted the card in his fingers while the gas poured. He had a good run with Britt, but this whole thing had gotten very weird. A new person in Vegas. Tony knew who that was, but he was too pissed off to break the news to her that she would soon be getting a call. And why so insistent about Tahoe? There was nothing there but a second-rate hideout. Was his boy leaving town?

Tony knew very little about the plan, but it was becoming more clear Britt was very tied to what happened today. All of the tragedy and loss. Tony had a cousin who died in a firefight in Afghanistan after September 11. He still hated that whole chain of events. Tony may have been a life-long criminal, but he wasn't a fucking terrorist. He had a boy in Los Angeles who could hook him up with work. Suddenly, that sounded a lot more inviting than Tahoe. He could stay in Britt's pad on the coast there tonight and then disappear tomorrow before Britt even knew. He had contemplated this moment for some time, but that last bloodless call did it. You always needed an out in his business.

Clean up your own mess, Britt. Take the pepper spray yourself. Kill your own crazy bimbo. She was better than you anyway. See you in the next life.

FORTY-TWO

Britt had known this was going to be a problem. Why could he not control his feelings? Feelings had always been easy for him. He thought at times he became immune to them. But now, at the worst possible time, here they came: anger, betrayal, confusion, impotence. He was the king of the fucking world, and yet he couldn't control his own erection.

This rage, though—maybe this rage would do it. He went back upstairs. The girls were there, cooing, nuzzling, kissing with each other. It was nothing worse than you would see on Cinemax. Priscilla kissed Jilly's neck. Her back was arched, feeling it, taking in the moment. Tilly smiled when she saw Britt. She motioned for him to join them.

"We've been waiting," she said in a practiced but effective purr. He lay down and they all moved to him. This was power.

Tilly undid his shirt, button by button. She flung it open like something out of a rock video and kissed his nipple. He knew it was supposed to be sexy, and it was. But nothing happened.

Root canal, deposition, random errands—they were just as stimulating to him. His breathing grew stronger. The girls figured he liked it, but the whole endeavor was making him nervous. He wasn't moved by this fantasy that most men would give years of their life for. These girls were all his and would give him any wish. Priscilla could sense something wasn't right. She grabbed his crotch—should-be heaven, but still nothing.

What was wrong with him? What was wrong? Fuck, what moved the needle? What did he need to have to make him powerful? He knew. He had it right there. He stood up and moved across to the other side of the room.

He got his gun.

FORTY-THREE

Raylon for Becky—by the time they got back to Hollywood, that was a trade Joey was very happy to make.

During the last fifteen minutes of the car ride, Becky couldn't shut up. The shock of the explosion had worn off, and she huffed and puffed about who she gonna call and what they gonna say about all dis shit. After telling her twice not to tell anyone he was alive, Joey figured out he was better off *not* emphasizing this; she was clearly the kind of girl that did something just because someone didn't want her to.

He let her out just about four blocks from where he had found her, winked at her, and told her he would call. They both knew he wasn't going to, but he had to say it if there were any chance it would help her shut the hell up.

Becky got out, Raylon climbed in, and Marvin drove the pair away while Becky made loud noises so that everyone would notice what a fancy car she had gotten out of. She was sure she could keep

Joey's secret. She knew something that no one else in the world knew.

Raylon was hurt but knew he couldn't show it to Joey.

Joey felt horrible but knew he couldn't say anything to Raylon. They sat on opposite sides of the limo, looking like freshmen who had just gotten invited to a formal with the upperclassmen. They said nothing and barely moved.

Marvin ended the silence by asking where they were going. Joey told him to head toward the beach. He didn't intend to end up there but figured they would almost certainly end up going west.

"How the fuck we get paid to get killed?" he finally asked.

Raylon still seethed about the whole afternoon but to accuse him of being the reason for this? Incredible. He knew he could say more than anyone else, but, frankly, that wasn't much these days. He shook his head and didn't make eye contact, hoping Joey would get the idea.

"Man, you remember? You remember anything? I *told* you not to do this. I *told* you this was bad news. This tha one you made me get in cash."

Joey looked at him as if they had never laid eyes on each other before.

Raylon chuckled in disbelief. "Shit. They came to us last month. You say we don't know them, they ain't regular industry. I said it ain't worth it. You said get the money in cash."

It was obvious this didn't register with Joey. Raylon thought he was playing dumb.

"So I met the guy. He gave me fifty in cash then, and then gave me fifty in cash two days ago. Same guy. Italian or some Mediterranean motherfucker. It's what we went to the strip club on."

Now Joey nodded. He remembered that. He made it rain like a tropical storm.

"Bitch ask me, you there too? He knew I saw something.' I don't think I saw him, but he knew I knew something.' I sure as hell know where he live."

Joey's eyes got big. "You know where he live?"

"I followed him. I knew nothin' was right."

"Raylon, you my nigga."

"I don't wanna talk about it right now, man. I don't wanna talk about it. We gots a score to settle. Tell me where we need to go."

It was the one thing they could agree on.

FORTY-FOUR

Mandy relayed word to Grant. They were going to Vegas. They called Caitlin and made arrangements to meet her near the airport. Mandy made Grant place the call on speakerphone so she could hear both sides of the conversation. He could hear the trepidation in Caitlin's voice. Grant thought Naseem was affected by the call as well, as he now appeared to be constantly frowning.

They headed to the airport. Naseem looked more perturbed than he was previously. When Mandy took a phone call, Naseem motioned to him. He needed a moment alone with him.

"Something just hit me," he whispered while Mandy kept talking. "Check your bank account."

Grant stared at him. "What?"

"Just do it."

Grant was about to say something back, but he didn't want to tip off Mandy. Naseem still hadn't disappointed him; every bit of

159

information was gold.

He pulled his cell phone out of his pocket and went to his banking app. Grant put in his password and scrolled to the accounts screen. He quickly put the phone in his pocket as they navigated the tarmac and were let out to get on the jet.

He looked at Naseem as they boarded the plane. Naseem's look said he had figured it out. He didn't need to tell him. Grant went into the air knowing that his account had just had a deposit made just that afternoon. That morning, he had checked it. It was quite healthy, just short of six figures.

Now it held ten million dollars.

FORTY-FIVE

He marched halfway back across the room before they knew what was going on. Priscilla stood up and tried to reason with him. Jilly and Tilly sensed that wasn't going to help, and they scattered to the corners of the room. That left him with Holly, beautiful, lithe Holly, who was now frozen in the middle of the bed, looking at him with terror, which almost did it for a minute. Could he build on that? He closed his eyes for a second and listened to her whimper. It was close to making him hard but not enough. He pulled the gun up and shot her.

Blood went wild. It covered Jilly, who was too close to the bed to avoid it. The others screamed but stood still, not knowing if it was better to run or to freeze.

Britt looked at Priscilla, who was trying to hold his gaze.

"Let's try this again."

FORTY-SIX

Becky thought about it. Joey had told her that it could be dangerous for him if the world knew he was alive. But they needed to! All of her friends who had met minor rap stars like Wocka Flocka Flame and Twista would be crazy jelly if they knew her part in history! She was with the fucking Pal during all of this! What luck.

But surely she could be down, keep his secret, right?

And then it hit her. This shit could get her on TV and make her some money! Her nails didn't French tip themselves.

She knew he'd be mad, but Joey would get over it. She was sure of this.

She pressed the on button. Then she saw it: Joey had slipped out the battery. She wondered if he had seen the picture she took.

FORTY-SEVEN

Caitlin soaked in the news. They were coming: Grant, Naseem, and Mandy, who had so opportunistically taken Grant's job in the wake of the scandal. She shook her head as she realized that even now she was taking up for Grant even after all he did to her.

She remembered how perfect that summer was: seeing the man she loved mature in every way, taking those fancy trips, and finally loving her job, mainly because she was so preoccupied with everything else. It was the most magical time of her life. She got to fly to meet her future husband who was protecting the *president*, and she had gotten the romantic proposal on the beach, the exact way any girl would want it to happen. It seemed too good to be true. For three weeks, it was.

Their picture had appeared in the papers in a manner befitting the minor celebrity Grant was. She showed her ring to everyone she knew, and together they celebrated in a way that only women can do over a perfect proposal.

She floated across the ground. Nothing could touch her, or her man, or her happiness.

And then she woke up on a Saturday morning in late August. She didn't get a warning call and had no sense of foreboding. She just turned on the television, flipped through the channels, and thought, "I know that head."

That head belonged to her fiancé, and it was being displayed in a cell phone shot laying across a set of breasts. Both her fiancé and the owner of the breasts were naked and completely passed out. Unfortunately for everyone, the breasts' owner was Saudi royalty.

But oh, there was more. The same intrepid photographer also had a grainy and backlit video of the pair doing the nasty in a VIP room at some Washington nightspot. You couldn't tell it was them exactly except that it appeared to be taken at the same nightclub. The photo, though, left no doubt that Grant Miller was an asshole, creep, and philanderer.

No one had any comment. The political scene was tense, knowing how big this scandal could be. It appeared Grant Miller, FBI playboy, had just defiled one of the most famous virgins in the world and one of the few women whose sexual status could disrupt the diplomatic standing of nations.

It was everywhere. Take-no-prisoners reporters came and camped out on her lawn by late that morning. They shouted at her. When she ignored them, they shouted louder. She had no comment. They didn't care. They kept asking questions, and she became a zombie. Grant called. She didn't answer. She texted him and told him she would ship his stuff back to him, and she was keeping the ring. Well, she was selling the ring.

Her family tried to help, but there's a time when you need

help, and there's a time when you don't want anyone to touch you, or speak to you, or even acknowledge that you exist. That was what Caitlin wanted.

The reporters camped for a few days, but then they finally figured out she wasn't going to be any fun, wasn't going to play the jilted lover in front of their lenses. They wanted potshots at Grant, but she wasn't going to give them that; he did enough to embarrass them both.

The first few days, this was front page news—an international incident with sex, fame, money, and privilege. But behind the scenes, the other princess, her sister, lobbied her father. She saw Grant and the princess together. She saw nothing wrong; she had actually heard Grant speak fondly of his new fiancée. She believed that the pair had been drugged.

She knew her sister well enough to know she was about as virginal as your average call girl, and she also hadn't seen anything to indicate Grant made any advances. She made her father watch the video, which she showed him did not in any way definitively indicate it was them as participants and not someone else, and she single-handedly saved Grant's job.

President Bush, who considered Grant almost a buddy, put in a stern call after he had cleared things with the Saudis, indicating Grant was to be placed on leave but not fired, which was tantamount to a miracle.

Grant had relayed all of this information to Caitlin in a series of long-winded e-mails. While it may not have been enough evidence to convict him in a criminal court, it was more than enough to make the woman who had let him hold her heart despise him forever.

He called once or twice a month still, two years later. He asked friends to tell her hi. He acted like the most clueless man in

America or someone who was truly innocent.

She still agonized over all of this. She mourned their closeness. But she couldn't bring herself to believe that some conspiracy theory had surrounded their relationship to tear them apart.

Caitlin headed west. She took up bad habits she had never had before but adapted to quickly. In college, she was the life of the party. She was known as a party girl, but that was all a calculated facade. She could hold her liquor, and she knew how to pretend around drunk and high people. It wasn't hard.

Now, she drank like she was racing her liver down the drain. She dialed random phone numbers in Grant's area code in the middle of the night. She never got the number right on purpose. She left rambling messages on random voicemails, lashing out at Grant without ever speaking to him.

She did cocaine and ecstasy like she was the long-lost child of Hunter S. Thompson. She stayed up for days. The rational Caitlin asked herself why this one man did this to her. There was only one answer she could give: she had trusted him with every inch of her life.

She had allowed herself to be put into the spotlight, and he had destroyed her, pulled the chair out from under her. She was a national laughingstock along with him. She was the dumb girl to be pitied. She had trusted him, and he had thrown her to the curb.

She threw herself headlong into one self-destructive relationship after another, but she trusted none of them. She had none of that to give. She quickly figured out that there were plenty of men in Vegas who would pay to have you around.

That's what she became: the arm candy that you most likely weren't taking home. Oh, she was a good sport and would let all of your friends think you were sleeping with her, but she still was too conflicted to be a slut. She was just a bad, bad drunk who liked to stick anything up her nose. She put herself into compromising positions, like the one with the cowboy. But somehow, she had managed to make it to this point physically intact. That might just have been a miracle.

Then she got pinched. One of her benefactors was a coke dealer named Randy, and he sent her to make a delivery. It was a sting, and she wound up on her knees in a foyer with a DEA gun next to her temple and a possession with intent to distribute rap next to her name. She was looking at a long stint in federal prison.

This, too, she felt was Grant's fault. He was the cause and the source of her fall, from the first sip to the final nadir. She didn't even think like this before him. Now, she was afraid to tell her family and sure she was going to wind up gone for a long time. How she would return was anybody's guess.

Then she learned the power of the payoff. Randy came in, displayed actual human emotion, and got her out of the charge. She was sure there were payoffs; she was guilty as sin after all and caught in the act. But her lawyer handed her the dismissal, and she certainly didn't ask any questions.

After that, her behavior became more reckless instead of less. She was still a fun drunk's favorite fun drunk, but the nights dragged on too long. She became belligerent and violent. She could match you two shots for one. She got you thrown out of places. She threw the occasional glass and caused memorable scenes. She hoped to never have to hear from her conscience or her heart again. She raged against him and used his name like the vilest curse word. But she never threw away his number. She always knew he was her final safety net.

And now, she had to use it. Once she started questioning Britt's motivations, she thought back to all the questions he asked her about Grant. Everyone was interested once they found out about her involvement in what was the scandal of the summer of 2008. But Britt asked weird, specific questions. Lots of them.

Was this all tied to that horrific mess? Had her man been set up as he had tried telling her, crying to her on a thousand voicemails? After years of utterly discarding that thought, it suddenly didn't seem so far-fetched.

FORTY-EIGHT

On what seemed like the longest day of his life, President Morgan suspended all air flight until Friday morning, leaving him about six hours to deal with the stock exchange deadline of 3 a.m. Friday morning, Washington time.

The stock was trending up. The timing by Sabotage didn't give anyone much time to think, and it appeared that many citizens felt they were doing some sort of civic duty by placing orders. The SEC looked into how many orders were placed by computers infected by the virus. President Morgan had conferred with the prime minister of Japan, and the Japanese had agreed with the decision not to suspend trading. They felt that if the repercussions were too dire, both countries and both leaders stood to face serious backlash and future pressure if a terrorist could simultaneously control national security and the markets. Morgan went over this decision, and he still wasn't fully convinced he was making the right choice, but he could always play the card that it wasn't his index to stop. That was chickenshit, but you did what you could to make it out alive of this type of situation.

He didn't like to conduct business in the Oval Office, because it felt like such a church. He told anyone who wanted to hear he felt like he was fingering Dolly Madison if he did anything too serious there. But he was tired and cranky and felt silly moving them all back downstairs to have another briefing that was not going to move anything along. So he beckoned them all to sit and hoped they had more answers than the last time. He saw Vanessa raise her eyebrows as she knew his preference for the briefing room.

"Any leads at all?" Morgan said this as if all federal agencies were having a tea party all day. He directed it at any of the five staffers who were breathing the air in his office.

Only Vanessa was brave enough to answer. "Nothing solid. We are running all people who have active roles as if they are involved. That includes our agents."

"Including Miller?"

"Especially Miller."

"Anything yet?"

Vanessa shook her head. "No, his personal accounts checked out fine. But it looks like he may do most of his business through some corporation he started when he was booking a lot of appearances and receiving speaking fees. His personal account has just a few hundred dollars in it. His paycheck isn't deposited there. We're trying to work with his bank to get the rest of his records, but there are other names on the accounts, so we may have to get a search warrant."

"Well shit. Don't spend too much time on that. I can't imagine it's him. I don't think he's that bright. I've met him a couple of times."

In fact, Morgan met him more than that. Just like his

predecessor, he loved Miller. He had also put in a good word with the director after all of the mess he put them all through. Miller sat at a dozen ceremonies with him, and he had seen enough of him to think of him as a big, football-loving lug. He really couldn't imagine him befouling any princesses, and he certainly couldn't see him being meticulous or ruthless enough for this. He frankly still considered Miller a hero. He hoped he wasn't wrong.

"Miller's not the primary target, but the wrinkle of his girlfriend popping up does make it a little more interesting."

Morgan nodded. He would need a lot more convincing.

"Did the bomber have any information?" the president asked, more resigned than curious.

"He ties the man he calls Yankee to Las Vegas and Los Angeles. People-wise, his was a small operation if he's telling us the truth, and what he has said has checked out so far. He placed several of the explosives himself and sent the packages that brought down our airliner. We're running scenarios, but we believe there's little additional air traffic danger, so we can probably resume that in the morning just after we've swept for more packages from the companies which now appear to have been bought by this group for shipping packages for today."

Morgan was known for being bold. He loved his reputation as a cowboy, but he didn't have enough info to take any bold steps at all. He was tied up and only a few hours from a deadline that made him very nervous.

FORTY-NINE

After they sat in the air for an hour or so and after she was done with her numerous conversations with FBI personnel in DC, Mandy asked Naseem if he would give Grant and herself some privacy. He nodded, none too pleased, and looked like he was passing kidney stones as he went up to sit in the back.

Mandy sat down and placed her hand on Grant's arm. He was taken aback. He was still thinking about the money. He did not want to have anything to do with this conversation. It was going to either wind up being some soul-baring awkwardness, or yet another ass-chewing, or worse, his Miranda rights. He needed none of these right now.

"Grant, I have something to confess."

He had no idea where this was going, but it looked like it was heading toward awkward. He just prepared his best poker face and went along with it.

"I never thought you did it."

"Did what?"

"I never thought you did anything wrong with the princess."

This made his blood boil. He considered Mandy a friend, semi-close at the time, and when the entire world took a piss on him, her friendship seemed to vanish. He saw her change from an ally who loved to hear about his latest adventure to someone who couldn't meet his eyes and couldn't believe her luck that things had so changed in her favor.

"Why are you telling me now?" he managed.

"Because I feel bad about it every time I walk by you. I had to create a distance between us. If I would have been seen as supporting you, I never would have gotten the job."

She was right about that. This job paid tens of thousands more a year. She didn't have a book contract and speaking fees. He couldn't begrudge her that.

"But I wanted it to seem real, so I just ... created it. Just eliminated you."

"Well, you did a good job," he managed. He turned one corner of his mouth up. He knew she wasn't telling the whole story. She might have come to realize he hadn't done it, but she hadn't been blameless in this. She fell into the judgment just like everybody else. He wanted to see where this was going. He shrugged. "A lot of people did that. You had good company."

She rolled her eyes. "That doesn't make it right. I'm offering you an apology."

He had trouble looking at her. "Look, I know I was radioactive. It's all over now."

Mandy traced the edge of her wristwatch with her right hand and looked up.

"That's the thing. I don't think it is over. Before tonight ends, I think somebody's going to try to pin this on you."

Grant swallowed. That was not what he was expecting her to say, although, after seeing his new bank balance, he believed this, too. He tried to keep the poker face but had no idea how badly he was failing.

"Why do you think that?"

"I don't know. It's all just too tidy. You get the lead; you get the call from your girlfriend … it's certainly managed to bring you back to the spotlight."

He threw his hands up—unbelievable. "You don't believe …"

She stopped him. "No, I don't believe. And maybe I'm wrong, but I know that you're not a traitor. You were a damned fine asshole agent who got caught up in reading his press and became an insufferable prick, but you were still a good agent. I have a sense this is coming down … on you."

"What are you going to do?"

"We're landing in half an hour. I'm going to think about how bad what I'm thinking about is going to screw me. If I can convince myself it's not half as bad as I'm thinking, then I'll tell you my plan."

Grant nodded. He had no idea if this meant she knew about the money. He was almost as far out on a limb as Naseem, and it wasn't going to be any better any time soon.

FIFTY

I t took most of the rest of Becky's money to buy the cell battery, but it started the phone right up. There it was, waiting for her. She pulled the phone in close to her chest, and then put it on silent.

She had managed to get a shot of Joey without him knowing it.

She left them 45 minutes ago. That was long enough, right? This was seriously good shit. This was bangin. She was gonna blow up on Twitter.

She wrote the message:

@RachelXOXO—U wont believe dis shit. @PalJoey alive! I wuz wit him in his limo.

She added hashtags about Pal Joey to make sure it would reach its intended audience, and she posted a link to the picture she took. Joey looked a mess, dealing with the issue, and panicked, almost white. It wasn't a flattering picture, and it certainly would lead anyone to guess exactly when it had been taken. If they doubted, the timestamp would clearly show that.

It didn't take long. Within five minutes, she had direct messages from CNN, TMZ, and BET. Shit was blowing up. Rachel, known as Becky to Pal Joey, was about to become famous.

FIFTY-ONE

Raylon had been to the house twice, but he knew he would have to feel his way up to it, especially in the dark. He gave the driver general directions, taking surface streets through Bel Air and Beverly Hills, and then heading north on Coldwater Canyon Drive. With the windy, narrow roads, he knew this was not fun driving for a limo, but, at this point, all involved were still pretty content with simply not being dead.

The canyons were not places you went if you didn't know where you were going. They twisted back upon themselves, and you could easily wind up going into a blind alley with no way to turn around. Neither Raylon nor Joey claimed to be an expert on this ritzy part of Los Angeles that seemed a million miles away from their neighborhoods in Dago. But Raylon always paid attention, and Joey knew his boy could find it.

Raylon had the driver cut back west onto Mulholland Drive, and then he started counting the streets. He told him to go slowly.

He finally found the cul-de-sac he wanted. No one expected the owners of the house to be home, and Joey figured they were armed to the teeth if they were. But they were in no hurry; they could wait.

He told Marvin to park up the hill in a darkened driveway across the street. The canyon streets were so narrow, and a white limo didn't provide much cover, but what could they do? There was a fifty-fifty chance the man would come back from the other direction, but this was LA, and limos blended in better than they did anywhere else in the world.

"You sure dis it?" Joey asked.

Raylon nodded. "I'm sure. What's the play?"

Joey sat silent for a minute. "You think dis the head man?"

Raylon shook his head vigorously. "Naw, man. He takin' orders."

"What make you say dat?"

"First off, I don't think I woulda seen his face if it's him. Just make sense, ya know? Second, it's just too big. He ain't runnin dis out of Laurel Canyon."

Joey tended to agree.

"So what's the play?" Raylon was enjoying seeing Joey squirm. He knew his days as a drug dealer were nearly worry-free because of the protection Raylon's group offered. Had they stayed on the streets, they would be partners by now. As it was, the rap game turned him into a permanent flunky.

Joey knew Raylon saw him as weak. This burned him.

"I'ma make him talk," he said forcefully.

Raylon gave him a knowing grin that only he could get away with.

"I know what ya thinkin,' " Joey said, staring straight at the only man who knew him this well. "I got dis."

Raylon remained unconvinced. He pulled out a fat blunt and offered it to Joey.

Joey hit it hard. He needed that. He then got the courage to turn on his phone just for a minute to see what the world was saying. His phone was blowing up off the hook. They were saying he was alive! Where was he? It took him a second, and then he saw. That damn Becky. She had gotten out over Twitter after all.

FIFTY-TWO

O nce the reports of the bombings came, Red knew the call
would come, eventually. Not everything could go right
on a day like today, and she knew she was still into Britt
enough to have to clean up the mess.

Red was at The Spearmint Rhino, not working as a dancer but
ready to roll the next white-collar Joe she saw. It was the nicest of
the Vegas strip clubs and looked more like a well-appointed law
office than the joint it really was. She tipped the doormen well to
overlook her occasional appearances, and there were so many girls
on the floor at any one time she was almost overlooked in the midst
of it all.

Frankly, she didn't exactly look like Mother Teresa. Her hair
was so red it was crimson. She helped it from a bottle now and
then, but, other than that, it was her. The ultimate redhead. She
played it up, too, wore the color, lived the lifestyle. She had to be
careful in her line of work, because she stood out, but she liked

that. It made it more challenging, certainly.

Time passed, and Red thought she was almost out of the woods.

Steve from Philadelphia thought she was a dancer. He sat down by her and made the rookie mistake of showing her his roll. Insecure men always make that mistake.

She cooed at him, told him she loved to watch the ladies, and watch the men watch the ladies.

He liked this. They always did. His eyes went up and to the right, the way people's eyes always do when they're conjuring up a pleasant image.

Red let him buy one drink, and then another. She was sure he was a lightweight. She was well into her beguiling act, a dance of talk, not of motion and always profitable.

Then Britt called.

She didn't answer.

He called again, and she still didn't answer. Then he came with texts and started blowing up her phone in earnest.

She kept two cell phones with her. They were identical except for the scratches and the rings. He was the one of the few people who had the number to her real phone. She didn't always bring it, but she was almost sure that by the end of the night she would have to do something extravagant and stupid.

"Excuse me," she told Steve, cursing Britt's timing to herself. "Girl talk." She winked and put her hand on his inner thigh. She grabbed Steve's phone, put her other number in, and sent a winky face. Her phone chirped as she received it.

He liked all of this. They always did.

"What a surprise," Red said when she got into the bathroom. There were two girls doing lines on the bathroom sink. She rolled her eyes and pretended like she didn't notice. "Your plan didn't turn out perfect."

He simmered. "One loose end."

"I'm guessing the girl. They're the only thing that gets a man like you killed."

Britt didn't want to admit this, but he had to. "I can't find her. She figured out that the phone she was given was bugged. Or she's visited every Oriental sex parlor and jack shack in the last two hours."

"She's a smart girl, too smart to stay with you." Red was beholden to Britt, but she still wasn't going to kiss his ass. "Where do you think she is?"

He paused. "I think she's at the casinos. The bigger, the better."

"Tony can't find her?"

"Last I saw, Tony was heading for Los Angeles. He apparently thinks I'm stupid."

"So you're two for two. The one you knew was smart is smart, and the one you knew was dumb is dumb."

"He doesn't know he's being followed."

"That sounds easy. Why don't I take Tony?" She didn't think Britt knew about her relationship with Tony. She was sure Tony wasn't going to shit in his own nest.

Britt laughed. It sounded forced as if he were trying to hide his fear from his formidable friend. "Tony's under control."

This made her heart sink. She didn't want to see Tony hurt.

The girls walked out of the bathroom, sniffing up the party favors and preening. She had the place to herself.

She dug the knife in. "And you want me to find the one who's in the wind in a casino. That really narrows it down."

Britt said nothing. He knew she would understand. They hung up.

Red checked the iPhone clock. There was still time to have a little fun before heading out.

She texted Steve. *Meet me. Ladies room. Second stall.*

The smiley face was only seconds behind.

FIFTY-THREE

Naseem, now by himself, had time to ponder the day. He woke this morning thinking this was his last; that had been a freeing experience most of the world would never know. Now, he was once again caught in an earthly narrative, no matter how short, and it weighed him down in a way he couldn't have expected.

He wanted to find Yankee. He wanted to kill him. Grant and Mandy did not want to know the lengths he was willing to go. Whether the rest of the plan was carried out or not, his motive was strictly revenge—making Yankee pay for perverting his mission, or that's what he tried to keep telling himself. There was part of him that wondered if he wasn't really okay with what happened, this endorphin rush, or his life somehow restored. He wasn't sure.

Naseem saw that Grant and Mandy were slightly wary of him. Grant tried that weak bluff of kicking his ass, but, overall, the Americans treated him with more kindness and respect than he ever could have hoped or deserved given the horrible things he meant to carry out. They would have both been killed by his hand if he hadn't reached out. That was a trait that his people didn't share. They would never have saved their potential killer. Even if it were to their great detriment, Naseem, had he done the same thing in his organization, would have been killed by the rules of his own people.

This weakness was Americans' greatest strength, he thought. They sometimes did a horrible and misguided job, but they thought they cared about right and wrong, and they wanted to see right done. Moreover, they wanted to *believe* they had done right. At least, this was true of the people themselves; their organizations sometimes lacked their people's vision.

He doubted that Yankee was still in Las Vegas, but he knew where to look, and he hoped something there would give him some insight. Yankee fooled him; only his last interaction prior to going to Missouri and his sanguine nature gave him any more than a slight pause. He believed this was the only time as an adult this happened. He always judged people well. He knew it would not happen again.

He had spent his last several years waiting for this, for the day he would no longer exist on this planet, only in the welcoming arms of Allah. He knew the scriptures, chapter and verse. He thought he could end this ringing pain of existence that everyone suffered and fall away. He would be a part of something bigger than himself. That feeling of loneliness that enveloped him every morning would no longer touch him.

Now, he couldn't say for sure that was what he wanted. He told Grant he wanted to die, but he knew it was highly unlikely that an American, who foolishly valued life too greatly, would do this. He still wanted this, maybe more, now that he was drowning in the consequences of his actions that day. Could he do it himself? He knew enough to not know that answer. What was worth saving? What was worth fighting for?

He knew one thing: Yankee's death and humiliation was worth almost any price. That was worth living for. He would see him flinch. He would hear him scream—no matter what. After that was anyone's guess.

FIFTY-FOUR

There is no one more vulnerable on the planet than a naked male.

Red learned this long ago. She remembered her two years waitressing, during a series of poor decisions, at a place where the men smelled like their bad habits and treated her like a pincushion.

She learned how to turn that situation around.

Step One: appeal to their ego. This was the easiest. For all the talk of women falling for the slightest compliment, Red found that men were much easier to bring down. A wink and a nice word followed by a gentle touch on the thigh could bring any heterosexual man as far as she needed to get, which led to …

Step Two: appeal to their organ. Even when a man can control his sex drive, this becomes the primary focus of his life. Here is a man who can control his penis—those men, Red learned, are all famous for this ability. Everyone else needed to rub one out on or near her, no matter any age difference. This led to …

Step Three: get them naked, keep them naked, and you can have whatever you want.

On this evening, Red opened the door to the ladies' room slightly, crooked her finger at Steve, and shut the door behind him. She grabbed his tie and practically threw him into the middle stall. She kissed him violently, her tongue like a dagger, giving him no ability to control anything. She took her time to bait the trap, no matter how much she hated kissing these ciphers. She put her mouth against his ear, said nothing but breathed often, and then ripped his shirt apart, sending the buttons flying across the room. She bit his neck, hard.

He started to unzip his pants.

She laughed. "No, take 'em off."

"Can't I …?"

She grabbed him and bit his neck like she meant it this time. "Don't be a pussy." No man ever has ever liked being called a pussy. "If you're going to ride this, you're going balls out. I don't play." This half-concocted line never failed. No man could see the lack of logic on the other side. There had never been a bankroll yet big enough to keep the pants from being kicked into a heap.

She teased her short skirt up her thighs, showing him she was not wearing any underwear.

He could see the tattoo over top of her pubic bone, but couldn't read what it said.

She turned around and raised her ass and moved it back toward him. Then she turned suddenly again and grabbed the shirt and threw it over the stall. She winked at him and then changed her expression to a more serious look. She put her finger on his lips. "Hold it." She looked down to sell it. "Shit, let me grab a little friend." Red winked at him, and he bought it.

They always bought it. This man, who was probably good at his job and not terribly reckless and most likely good with other people's money, left all of that self-control at the sight of her thighs. That man didn't exist for the time being.

She left the stall with Steve thinking she was grabbing a condom.

How wrong he was.

While Steve had his dick in his hand, Red gathered up all of his clothing, with the exception of his socks, which he was still wearing, and without saying a word, left the restroom. She stuffed the clothes in her oversized purse and told the first bouncer she saw with a dramatic flutter that there was a completely naked man in the ladies' room. She looked shaken. She made a vaguely Scarlett O'Hara gesture that just seemed right. This sent every bouncer into chivalry mode, and this one was no different. He strode toward the problem, and she left the premises and grabbed the first taxi she saw.

"7710 Constanso Avenue," she said and reached into her purse to count the money as the cab sped away. This was sport; now, she had work to do. She was going to pay her dear friend Caitlin a visit.

FIFTY-FIVE

The girls scattered, but there was nowhere really to run. He had the gun. Priscilla was fully nude while the other two were in bras and panties.

Priscilla was the brains. She edged up the wall to her full height from the crouch she was in. "What do you want from us?" She asked like a seasoned hostage negotiator. "I'm sure we'll do it. We're easy."

Britt felt the waves of emotion. They poured over him. It wasn't her fault. He was so ashamed. He was so helpless. Everything had gone. He worried that someone heard the shots. But if anyone came, he would shoot them, too. He thought he was far enough away that any noise would be excused—such was the power of privilege.

Then he felt the stirrings. It was working. The killing was returning his masculinity. "Come over here," he said to her. She was so much sexier, prettier, smarter than the others. "Make me hard."

"Then put the gun down." She inched toward him.

He didn't call her out.

She decided to continue. "Use your other gun."

He shook his head. "Not yet."

She pulled his pants down. Didn't look like he was working with much. She looked back to Jilly and Tilly and motioned them to join her.

Priscilla used her calmest voice. "Ooh looky here girls," she said, motioning with her eyes to the door. "Look at this."

She turned her head and bit his scrotum—hard and fully. She pulled down with her teeth and yanked with her mouth just to make sure he was hurt very badly.

He screamed like a three year-old, and blood spurted everywhere.

"Run girls," Priscilla spat, knowing the chances of anyone getting out alive were slim.

Britt figured out the play mid-scream: she wanted him to deal with her first, giving the other two time to escape. The pain returned him to his senses. The FBI training kicked in. He wheeled and shot both of the women in the head.

They didn't have time to make a sound. They didn't reach the door.

He looked down and saw the blood. It was bad. He turned back to Priscilla. "You didn't have to do that."

"But I'm glad I did," she said. Her face was covered in his blood.

He thought about shooting her in the kneecaps, making her pay for the pain he was feeling. But he needed fewer loose ends, not more. He overcame the rage and shot her once but deadly enough. She was no longer a problem.

Britt went to the bathroom to see what he could do about his wound. He jumped in the shower and watched blood pour off him. The wound wasn't as bad as he expected. He had some bandages in his overnight bag and luckily a change of clothes. This would hurt like a mother, but there was nothing that wouldn't heal.

He couldn't believe it. He wasn't right. He was concentrating on all the wrong things while so close to the payoff for all his hard work. He was obsessed with his dick. What was wrong with him?

He sat on the bed to fix his dressing. Oh, did it hurt, but the bleeding was almost stopped. If she moved left or right an inch or two, it would have been much worse. He thought of Monty Python—only a flesh wound, indeed.

Britt found a pair of dark jeans and a red shirt. It was the best he could do about hiding the bleeding if it were to restart. He would just have to take his chances and soldier on.

He turned the air conditioner down all the way and put the Do Not Disturb sign on the door. He hoped this would buy him enough time. He needed to be out of Vegas very soon.

He called his driver and told him to meet out front.

FIFTY-SIX

Mandy had about five minutes to think this through. The plane was taxiing, and she would be met by other Fibbies as soon as they deplaned. She dispatched Naseem and Grant to the front of the plane fifteen minutes earlier to give her a moment by herself. She caught a knowing glance from Naseem that made her very uneasy. She could sense that the initial horror of his double-cross was wearing off, and his resolve was likely setting in. She didn't know if that led him in a different direction, but it was yet another thing that weighed on her.

Grant was being set up. She received an e-mail a few minutes before indicating that ten million dollars was transferred into his account this morning. Knowing what Naseem said, this fit perfectly with someone trying to hang the blame on him. He was part of a plan and either bungled the St. Louis explosion or was double-crossed, and now he was dead. The financial impact of this plot was obviously huge if someone could spend ten million dollars just to frame someone.

She spent half an hour e-mailing with Vanessa Jones about what to do. After giving her the go-ahead to make this crazy trip, Jones wanted to question Naseem and Miller separately—in custody. This seemed insane. There was no time to waste if Grant actually had a connection to someone who knew this villain and had spoken to him recently. Vanessa said other agents could check that out. Mandy knew how well that would work. Caitlin wanted and needed her connection with Grant. They had a shorthand, the way lovers and good friends do. Caitlin would become very unwilling to cooperate once she knew she wasn't working with Grant.

At one time, she was interested romantically in Grant. Who wasn't? He was an asshole, but all women love a rich, talented, good-looking asshole. They fight over them. She never acted on it, realizing it would be career death. Instead, she developed a buddy-buddy, frenemy thing that lasted until his famous public swan dive. Of all the things she had to reconcile, especially now, her complete Judas kiss of Grant was right up there.

Only three minutes to go. The airport was clear of departing flights, so it might be sooner.

They were arriving at McCarran Airport, private terminal, gate 7. She texted the agents to meet her at stall 17. It would buy them five minutes. With these two, she was sure that was all they would need.

She walked straight at Naseem and Grant, who were steeling for whatever was ahead.

"Boys, they think they're onto something. They're wrong. They can't hear ya, but they can see ya on that camera directly over the pilot's door." She made no motion.

They knew.

"I'm gonna sit down and look at my phone while you disable it."

Naseem stood and made a single gesture, putting his right thumb painfully into the center of the camera. He winced from the pain.

Grant saw blood, but there was no more camera.

"Tie me up, Miller. Stick something in my mouth. Wanted to say that for a long time." She winked at him.

He deftly obeyed her.

"They're coming from 17. They think you two are somehow in cahoots. Head the opposite direction. They'll let me go in an hour or two, and I'll text my phone." She motioned and Grant took it.

"Anything else?" Grant asked.

"Nope, give it to me."

Grant took a heavy blue dinner napkin from a serving tray and stuffed it into her mouth.

"Thanks," he said, knowing how much she was risking.

She winked at him again, knowing she might well be kissing her career goodbye. At least it wasn't another Judas kiss.

FIFTY-SEVEN

The revelation that big money had transferred to Grant Miller bothered the president. He knew it shouldn't, that Miller might have been bitter or worse for many years, considering the way he was treated, but it did bother him. He wanted to see Miller persevere and win; he did not want to see his name trampled any further.

He went back and forth with Vanessa about this several times. He believed they could bring Miller in, trace the funds, show he had nothing to do with this, and quietly take him off the case. He believed that whoever was responsible found an easy target in Miller, and, frankly, even if it was something worse than this, he did not want another scandal. Give the man a chance to walk out a side door and away from this drama.

Vanessa believed this was the president interjecting too much of his personal feelings. Miller was an agent and, at one time, a good one. He knew the pitfalls of doing the wrong thing; if he did so, let his ass hang out in the wind. This White House needed no more issues right now.

There was just over an hour until Sabotage's deadline. Bomb squads and other crews were scouring the grounds of Kenner Industries for any signs of foul play or possible explosives. The president was not interfering with the stock price and not closing the markets, but the American people propped the stock up at thirty-seven. If this was Sabotage's goal, he would have his short-term victory, but Vanessa was going to make it a personal goal to bring him down. If this was all about money, she would never let it go. Good people, including children, died today in a painful and indiscriminate manner. She would do whatever necessary to see him swing.

Vanessa had expected to hear something from Mandy by now. The separate interrogations should be underway. It had been over twenty minutes since she got word they landed. She palmed her phone and checked the e-mail again—nothing. She thumbed the antenna on and off just to make sure it was still working. Cell phones sometimes did strange things even one belonging to someone in her position. Still, there was no sign.

She looked down and read the latest FBI briefing. It mentioned the amount in Grant's account. Then something hit her—something she wanted them to follow up on.

Miller was more business savvy than most agents. He made some diversification of his assets, she learned earlier that day. He was not going to retire, but his finances were healthy, set up for long-term growth. She knew this because the agents were required to submit their accounts to full-time monitoring. Miller knew this and had supplied the information to the Bureau.

So why would Miller give that account to the Feds? It would be easy enough to set up a dummy account under a corporate name. Without a serious goof, there would be almost nothing that the FBI could do to find this if they went looking, and it certainly wouldn't happen the same day as the transfer.

Miller was a smart guy. It seemed totally out of character for him to ask that any bribe or reward money be put in this account. It was like cheating on your wife on your couch while she was at home. You were assuring your own defeat.

Mandy seemed hesitant when she told her what to do with the men. She was understated, but she believed Miller was being set up. The president still had his doubts. Maybe she was being overly harsh. Maybe there was a middle ground.

Just then, as she finished the report, the phone rang. It was Vegas.

Mandy was calling but not from her own line.

"Yes, Mandy."

Mandy sounded shaken. She hoped she was pulling this charade off for a very powerful audience. "I've got some bad news. Amin and Miller overpowered me. They tied me up. The other officers are looking for them, but I think they're gone."

So much for that theory, Vanessa thought as she tried to imagine how to tell the president.

FIFTY-EIGHT

Britt made it downstairs and was learning how to walk with his new infirmity. He had packed several damp washcloths around the injury and looked an absolute mess. He was feeling lightheaded, and he instructed his driver to find the nearest Whole Foods and run in to get him some food. He needed energy. He didn't want to check the dressing too often, but, man, it hurt. There were just certain places that were going to be stunningly painful for a long time. He knew he needed to get it checked for infection as soon as he could. Human bites were among the most gnarly things to fix. He told his driver to find someone who could give him something for all of this. Vegas was filled with backroom quacks. He needed to find one quick.

As his man moved back into Vegas traffic, Britt tried to get his mind off of the last hour—the blood, the dead girls, and the limp dick. He felt ashamed, and he knew he needed to feel something else. He decided to try to get his mind back on the impending deadline.

He liked the direction the stock was trending. By his calculation, it was worth a couple million dollars more for the stock to hit thirty-five, but that wasn't his main concern. The trading activity itself made him fifty million dollars while he was sitting in his chair. His five-million-dollar investment in the plot and the ten million he spent that week to make sure Grant's name was ruined forever seemed well worth it. He would take that return any day of the week.

But he was still not out of the country, and that was an issue. He didn't have a "forever" arsenal of computer tricks. He was one man with a lot of money, but he wasn't Fort Knox. He wrote a few more programs that would dazzle and injure, but Sabotage was created to get him on his way out of the country within 24 hours. That time was rapidly approaching. He felt a little like a gambler with a dwindling stack of chips. Before, he was going on mojo, but, now, he had to plan how to maneuver with the mayhem he left. It was not a fun place to be.

There were no concubines or indentured servants, and he still had favors to repay. He needed to plan for the longest window of time as possible. He made each one of these thoughts between winces and thinking about opening the dressings just to see how much damage was done. Any movement felt like death. He needed a place to regroup.

When Caitlin left, he had a strong assumption she knew there were plans afoot. He made a mistake in ordering Tony to bring her back instead of simply putting a bullet in her scalp. He knew that now. The phone tracking device that worked so well and let him pinpoint her in less than an hour was still circling Las Vegas. It was clear she had ditched it and put it in a cab. He had to figure that she pieced some of his plan together and knew he was more than just a jealous boyfriend. Would she go to the authorities? He wasn't sure.

Caitlin was a serious party girl. She didn't turn tricks, but she could rage with the best rock star. Chances were she was carrying at least coke, if not molly, and maybe even some pressed pills. As he said these things to himself, he again could not believe he had allowed himself to be so compromised. Even a smart, alluring party girl was still a party girl.

He had to assume she would go to the cops, especially if she thought Grant was dead. The media had played up the fact that St. Louis was hit and even added this was the location where the famed FBI playboy was thought to be working. He knew she still was unresolved about Grant; she couldn't look him in the eye when she talked about him.

He developed a rhythm to aid with the pain. Deep, protracted breaths worked best, and the road seemed smoother than it had. He knew it probably wasn't getting better, but he was learning to deal with it. He could live with that until he could just hit the skyways.

If Caitlin went to the police, he thought, they could start piecing things together earlier than needed. He wasn't worried about Tony, who foolishly headed in the wrong direction in the desert, still an hour or two from LA. He had already sorted that out. But Caitlin could bring the heat too close.

Red was on her way. She would be worth ten Tonys, but he still had one other card to play.

They stopped and pulled into a low-rent strip mall. Britt looked up, and his driver signaled that someone was going to meet them with a medical bag and some friends. That made Britt the happiest he had been in some time.

While he waited, Britt gingerly grabbed a laptop out of his

bag. It was one he hadn't used for a month, because it had one specific purpose. Six months ago, he had paid a college student a small fortune to reroute a completely different mobile internet signal, one far less secure and easier to manipulate than the one he had carefully devised for Sabotage. It was routed so that it mirrored in every way a connection from Little Rock, Arkansas. He had tested it several times on Facebook, with local maps and other applications, and every time it had shown him as being in a neighborhood in the south half of Little Rock. He had installed it for exactly this purpose. The kid thought it was about some sort of illicit porn connection, but, really, it was so much cooler than that.

Britt logged on to his e-mail account as FriendlyHenry. FriendlyHenry had a Facebook account, a Twitter handle, and had ordered several pizzas, all from different hotel rooms in Jonesboro and Fort Smith, Arkansas. He had ordered gifts from Amazon and Target and had written letters to Mike Huckabee. In other words, when they started asking questions about this tipster, he would appear genuine. They would eventually find this was the computer that had set up the shipping business American Securities.

He opened the e-mail form and addressed it to Gayle Nipstad, an FBI agent high enough up the chain to be able to quickly make waves. He knew she would be working, because he had hacked into their scheduling computer that very morning. He also addressed it to twelve other agents and the general FBI e-mail address so that it would seem more believable. He typed in all cap—FriendlyHenry always typed in all caps.

I'M IN ARKANSAS. I'VE BEEN PAID WELL. I CAN'T STAND THE THOUGHT OF WHY I WAS PAID SO WELL. CHECK OUT AMERICAN SECURITIES AND THE OMEGA JET TO FIGURE OUT THAT I KNOW MY SHIT. I HELPED HIM SET IT UP. PRETTY SURE THE GUY'S NAME IS BRETT OR BRITT. I CALLED

HIM BRAT, ALTHOUGH HE ALWAYS HAD ME CALL HIM YANKEE. HE HAS AN APARTMENT ON THE 29TH FLOOR OF TRUMP TOWERS, LAS VEGAS. HE HAS A VIEW OF THE MOUNTAINS. I CAN'T REMEMBER ANYTHING ELSE ABOUT THE PLACE.

He proofread, added a spelling mistake or two, and pressed send. The apartment was actually on the 34th floor, but they would figure that out. This would divert them for hours if not longer. If it really worked right, it would kill them.

Just then, the door opened and a short man in a polo that showed way too much of his gut brought in his medical bag and nodded at Britt. He didn't know what tone to strike, so his "Let me see," came out forced and almost comical.

Britt rolled his eyes, dropped his drawers, and prayed for anyone to stop the pain he felt.

FIFTY-NINE

Tony was almost back to LA. He got to enjoy the desert cooling off, the disintegrating sky giving way to night. He had nothing but his thoughts, and, at a time like this, he wished he didn't. He tried to listen to music, but nothing felt right. He didn't like or trust Britt. Britt was a pretty boy with a mean streak. Tony really didn't think Britt couldn't handle fighting in the trenches. He sized him up as having some sort of academy training, but Tony had actually been in the streets, first in New York City and then in Vegas. He was there when the collars were made. He had heard the cartilage break, not looked away soon enough as someone was putting a round into some unfortunate soul. He could outsmart the boy. He needed to grab a few things, and then he could be on his way. Tomorrow morning, he would start a new life. He would circle back to Vegas in a different vehicle, see if Red wanted to come with him, and be gone. He had a little money saved. That sounded good.

He stopped off at a convenience store, grabbed a cup of coffee, and got back in the SUV. He looked down and saw his cell phone was ringing.

"Hey boss," he intoned, trying to sound reasonably cheery. "Whaddya need?" He had checked once to see if Britt tracked his cell phone; he hadn't. He realized he hadn't checked this in some time and hoped to hell nothing had changed.

"Where are you?" This sounded cold as almost anything that left Yankee's mouth.

"I'm almost to Tahoe."

"Making good time, huh?" Yankee almost seemed to brighten.

This surprised Tony. He didn't know if he was being tracked or not. He guessed he wasn't.

"Yeah, I'll be there in ninety minutes or less." He would actually be back to L.A. in less than an hour as long as there wasn't traffic.

"Call me when you get there. I've still got lots for you to do." The coldness returned.

"No problem. I'll call and get my orders." Tony wished he hadn't said it. It sounded stiff and stupid and something he wouldn't say.

Again, the cold. "Do that. I'll wait to hear from you."

Tony ended the call. He was going to be glad to be loose of that motherfucker.

SIXTY

Naseem and Grant sprinted off the airplane and down the tarmac. Grant saw Gate 17 to the left and made a hard right, which put them closer to the exit. He saw a motorized help cart and used his FBI badge to commandeer it. They sped off and were out of sight before anyone came out of the other gate. He knew it wouldn't be a long head start, but it was probably enough.

Naseem sized up the situation. He had silently seethed since Grant took the shot at him back in St. Louis. He knew he deserved it, but that didn't make it any easier. Now, he might just have one shot to do this right, and he wasn't sure Grant would be willing to do what needed to be done.

Grant saw a bureau-issued SUV ahead and found a wedge seam where he could get them between another vehicle and the SUV. He was two steps ahead of Naseem and had completely let his guard down, probably after some serious concern about flying with him in general. Grant stepped to the driver's door, and Naseem saw his chance.

He rushed him like a hockey player putting a man into the boards and hit him just under the shoulders. He hit him forcefully.

Grant fell forward, unable to brace himself. His nose broke on impact with the thick glass.

Naseem reached in his breast pocket and grabbed his badge. He obviously looked nothing like the lilywhite image of Grant, but there was no denying the value of a real FBI shield, especially on a hysterical day like today.

Naseem was sure he knew how to find Yankee. And he wanted to be the first one to do so.

SIXTY-ONE

Red told the cab to wait for her and paid the fare up until that point. She threw in enough of a tip to know he wasn't going anywhere.

The apartments were nice—for young people working as dealers, pit bosses, and servers at the town's casinos. The kids there drove nicer Hondas and Acuras and made enough to start saving for a house. There was a big pool in the middle that was well-lit by lights below the water, making everything look dreamy.

Red could smell marijuana as she walked toward the other side of the complex. She passed two girls, probably twenty or so, who were sitting on their boyfriends' shoulders, trying to knock each other off into the pool, giggling as if they were the funniest things in the world.

She found the building and checked out the door. No one was around, and there were no cameras that she could see. She walked up to the second floor and got her lock pick out. She struggled with the lock, which was surprisingly good for this kind of building, but it still didn't take her long; it just seemed like it.

Red turned on one light as she entered the apartment and would turn it off as she turned on the next one. She did not expect Caitlin to be here, but she didn't know who else had a key, and she wanted to be able to hide in time if someone walked in.

Caitlin was a slob, which was not surprising. Red had met her a couple of times. She was alluring and a fun time waiting to be had by all. That was Red's summation. She could see why Britt would like her. But Caitlin had never gotten over the situation with her ex. That was obvious the minute she took a drink. He came up again and again. Red thought that Britt, with whatever human emotions he could actually conjure, did like this girl, and she could tell he hated the emphasis on the ex, the FBI guy.

She had heard reports earlier. The FBI was hit in the attacks. She doubted that was coincidence.

She couldn't take forever, and it seemed like there were not many leads—no pictures with friends and a few with family, but they looked out of date. There was a laptop she would take but nothing that jumped out at her in the bedroom or the living room.

She saw one thing in the kitchen that caught her eye, only because there were so few pieces of personal information. It was a name—Tonya Jamison—and a cell number. It also had the word "Harrah's" on it. Red decided to start there.

She grabbed the laptop and the latest stack of bills. She might have written on them. Tonya was her best lead. The meter on the cab was still running, and Red thought this was the best she was going to get. It wasn't much, but she had scored on much less.

SIXTY-TWO

The tip had come in via e-mail. It wasn't much in the way of tips, something about an apartment "being involved," but it had some level of detail, and the investigators weren't exactly bubbling over with leads.

Lee Gates thought about not getting a warrant and just walking over and seeing what was going on. But he thought better of it. He took the ten extra minutes, faxed the paperwork, and received a warrant for his troubles. This wasn't enough on any other day of the year to get a warrant, he was sure. But today, when everything seemed so monumental, it was apparently more than enough.

Lee grabbed his partner, who was working on the explosion out in one of the city's industrial areas. Originally, the thought from Jessica Prater and other investigators was that the blast was unrelated to the day's events, but now she wasn't so sure. There was some report that at least one body was found, badly disfigured, more than would have been expected in this kind of fire. She was seeing if there was any way to tie that property to the apartment they were going to visit. She could find no connections.

They made their way onto the strip and noticed how few people were outside. It never looked like that on the strip. It seemed like the cumulative effect of the afternoon's madness had pushed everyone indoors. That seemed strange considering agents had thought the interior of a casino to be its most vulnerable spot. For years, they had fretted about large-scale interior attacks, but it was no matter now. The foot traffic was negligible, and there were fewer cars, but they didn't seem like things she could complain about right now.

"I think the American location was blown up to cover something, not as a civilian kill zone like the others. I think this was his base."

Lee nodded. This was as plausible as anything else he had heard this day: this was a false flag attack, this was domestic terrorists, this was Islamic terrorists—the default after a dozen years of worrying about these attacks. Las Vegas had as much freedom and access to whatever bad you needed. It would be the perfect place to organize a terrorist attack.

Lee pulled up to the Trump, gave the keys to the valet, and badged him. The valet said he would keep their ride up front. Jessica showed her ID and the warrant to the man at the front desk, who quickly got help.

"We believe that we are looking for the apartment of this man. We believe his name is Britt." She showed him the picture they were circulating of Britt Vasher, who they would know as Britt Vance.

The manager asked for assistance from the doorman, who quickly recognized him.

"I saw him this morning. He's on 34."

They confirmed this information and the manager got a key and accompanied them up the elevator. They walked down the long hall, turning left and then right, and then saw the number: 3472.

Lee knocked on the door. "Police."

No answer.

He knocked harder. This time Jessica announced them.

Still nothing.

The manager turned the key in the door and quickly peeled off.

Nick and Jessica entered and saw what they had. They had a murder, quite possibly of the main suspect in all this destruction. You reap what you sow and all of that.

SIXTY-THREE

Pal Joey and Raylon parked across the street from the house and played some low-volume old school shit on the stereo. They couldn't risk the music being loud.

Still no sign of the gangster.

Raylon wanted to be home, but since that wasn't possible, he rolled down the privacy glass. "Marvin, get some rest. We gon' be here a while."

Marvin nodded. "I'll do that." He put up the glass.

Raylon looked at Joey. "You too, man. Catch some rest. We may need you in a while."

Joey shook his head. He couldn't look tired—even now.

"Naw man," Raylon urged. "Get some rest. For real."

Joey took a hit of the little bit of purple that was still in the car.

"Aiight, man, I will."

Raylon was all to himself for the first time in many hours.

SIXTY-FOUR

Grant had never let his guard down quite so spectacularly, and his body paid for it. He didn't know how long he had been out, but he didn't think it was long. Still, it was long enough for Naseem to be well on his way. He felt the blood running down his cheek, and the pain radiated up and down his neck. But those were the least of his problems. Now, Grant was doubly fucked as there was still video of him assaulting Mandy on the plane. He cringed when he discovered he didn't even have his badge.

He heard his phone ring; thank God Naseem hadn't taken that. It was Caitlin, giving Grant no additional time to wallow in his grief. Grant grabbed at the phone.

Caitlin told him to come to Harrah's and explained as best she could what wing she was in. She told him to call again when he was on site, and they could talk on house phones, which seemed safer to her. After everything that had gone on, she was terrified

Britt might still have some ability to track her. Her rational mind was sure this wasn't the case, but she wanted to hedge her bets.

Grant told her he could be there in twenty minutes. He was also pretty sure that if he waited much longer there would be a dragnet thrown across the city looking for him. He walked through baggage claim, which was nearly empty, and ran to the front of the taxi line, normally longer than a good lie but instead had only a few employees trying to make it to the other side of town. Grant flashed his wallet as a "badge" and gave everyone a dirty look who dared cross him. He had learned this trick years ago, and he looked just gnarly enough to pull it off. The Indian man who kept the taxi line was no match, and he gave Grant the first taxi.

The cab smelled of incense and clove cigarettes; it was overpowering. Any other day, Grant would have waited for another cab, but today he didn't have time.

"Hundred bucks extra if you can get me to Harrah's in fifteen minutes," Grant said to the driver

His driver was astonished. "Done," he nodded.

SIXTY-FIVE

Yankee was more important to Naseem than freedom. Ending Yankee's life was more important than keeping his. He was willing to do anything he needed to in order to avenge what happened today. So the next move was easy.

He saw another government-issued Chevy Suburban, obviously an FBI vehicle. He knew he only had seconds, but it was worth a try. The vehicle was still running, and its driver stood having a smoke a few yards away. He hadn't thought this through, but he edged toward the vehicle, out of the driver's sight. He imagined that even with today no one was planning on someone doing something quite so bold. Naseem walked up to the vehicle, put it in gear, showed Grant's badge, and headed out. He figured the badge bought him a few seconds, so he drove slowly at first and then floored it as soon as he was past the flabbergasted driver. He made the corner and knew he could get out in time to put some distance between him and another vehicle.

Naseem managed to keep hold of the phone he bought at Wal-Mart. He expected them to confiscate it, but they hadn't—thankfully. It was another sign Grant didn't have the makeup to do what needed to be done with Yankee. He was foolish to believe he ever had. He was the only one who stood a chance.

Now, the phone came in handy. He memorized all of Yankee's numbers, but he knew that Yankee would be carrying only one phone now—the secret phone, only given to those closest to him.

He drove fast and texted. Sue him. He sent a simple and direct message:

THIS IS NASEEM. YOU DIDN'T KILL ME.

He didn't have to wait long for the response.

HOW DO I KNOW?

Naseem took a second. He needed to make this quick.

BECAUSE I HAVE THIS #. BECAUSE YOU'LL KNOW MY VOICE WHEN YOU CALL ME.

Brilliant. Make him make the move. He knew it wouldn't take long.

The phone rang. Naseem answered it immediately.

"Who is this?"

"You know who it is."

He could hear the recognition on the other end.

"Wha …?"

"Your plans have failed, you two-timing sonofabitch. Your woman is still alive, and she's meeting with your enemy, the real reason you did all of this."

There was a long pause.

"Where are you?"

"I'm coming to find you. Let me know if you want to make it easy." Naseem hung up the phone.

SIXTY-SIX

Raylon nudged Joey, who had almost gone to sleep. They were in this position now for well over two hours. Raylon wondered if they weren't chasing ghosts. Well, obviously, they weren't. Here was their man.

They rolled down the window after he went by. He didn't acknowledge their vehicle at all and parked in the driveway, not bothering to use the garage. He got out of the SUV and activated the rear gate. He got a small black carry-on bag out of the back and then closed the door. The vehicle made the familiar yap-yap sound and yellow lights flashed.

Joey started to walk out of the limo, but Raylon put his hand on his arm. He looked at Joey. *Wait. See what he's doing.*

The man pulled his phone out of his pocket. He was looking for the door code. He fumbled for a second but then found it. He punched the code in carefully and hit the pound sign.

Tony heard a "whee" sound he immediately recognized. He

took only a step when the door blew apart in a violent burst. The man was enveloped in the flames. His phone flew out of his hands, and his head hit the ground hard.

Tony, who had planned and executed so many deadly bombings since he was a teenager, now experienced what one actually felt like; he felt the all-encompassing pain, the nerves flaring, then numbing, and the sense of hallucination and all-too-real at the same moment. He saw two black men approaching him fast. He wasn't sure if they were friend or foe.

SIXTY-SEVEN

Caitlin heard the phone ring and let out a sigh of relief. She gave Grant directions from the lobby up to the room and then waited the eternity it took for him to arrive.

She looked at Grant, saw the damage to his face. She hugged him and wouldn't let go. He didn't know how to play this, so he stood still and held on. She stood in that spot for an awkwardly long time.

Grant thought about saying something stupid like, "Fancy meeting you here," but he couldn't stomach it. He squeezed her tightly and then stood away from her. The reunion was over. It was time to get to work.

"What can you tell me?"

"I've dated Britt Vasher for about six months. It was nothing serious at first, but he kept pursuing me." She looked down. It was hard to tell her former lover this. "I finally started seeing him more and more. He was always very inquisitive about my past, which is kind of rare. Most guys don't ask much, you know? I found it odd. Finally, it was really awkward, actually, and he asked about you. And then after he brought it up, he couldn't stop asking about you. It was weird. It was one of the first things that kind of pushed me off."

"Do you have a picture of him?"

"Just one, and it's not a good one. I left my phone in a cab on purpose, because I figured he could track me." She went to the dresser and picked up a picture she left there. "It's not great, but it's some people I have known for a couple of years. He's the ..."

"... Second from the left."

Caitlin looked at him. "You know him?"

"His name isn't Britt Vasher. It's Britt Vance. He was one of the FBI agents I busted in 2006."

Caitlin's heart sank. This wasn't about her at all. It was about Grant.

"So he ..."

"Set me up in D.C."

Caitlin wanted to vomit.

Grant didn't have an I-told-you-so left in him. He had to figure out how to get this information to the FBI, who now wanted him.

"Whose phone is least compromised?"

Caitlin gave him the phone that Tonya gave her.

"No problem."

He looked at Caitlin. "Can your girl get rid of this after I'm done?"

"No doubt."

"Call her now."

Caitlin went to the room phone and did this.

Grant searched who to call. Mandy would be the easy choice,

but he didn't want to give her any more grief. He didn't really have friends in the last couple of years. He didn't have any of his contacts with him, so he decided to call the general FBI tip line in Vegas. He even had to search for this number.

After the dance of the automated phone, he finally got an operator. "This is Special Agent Grant Miller."

"You are wanted, Agent Miller."

"I know. I can't come home just yet. Need to find a couple more details. But I have one bit of information you need. The man to look for? His name is Britt Vance. He masterminded this whole thing." Grant wanted to say, "to get even with me," but he didn't. It sounded egotistical. It might not even be true. It probably seemed too flippant. But he knew that it was true, and it explained everything.

When he got off the phone, Tonya was waiting by the door. He handed her the phone she was going to make disappear.

SIXTY-EIGHT

Red promised more money to the cab driver if he could make it to Harrah's quick. She figured out her play. But first, she needed to help someone important.

Tony was the best lover she had ever had. He wasn't a great conversationalist, wasn't really great to even look at, but man he was well-equipped, and he could do what she needed. Red had always been horribly conflicted about sex. She used it as her stock-in-trade, but there were too many weird come-ons by a middle school teacher for her to feel completely comfortable with it. She couldn't orgasm without deep penetration from behind, and she memorialized her sexual difficulties with a tattoo just above her vulva that read, in a beautiful and enigmatic script, *You Tried.*

If you were able to read her tattoo, you were not in position to take care of her. And, really, only Tony could do this reliably, from behind, with great effort, and intensity. Britt had no business fucking with Tony. That was her job. And by the way, Britt knew what he had in Caitlin: fucking trouble—beautiful, wild, fucking trouble. That was his fault, not Tony's.

If Tony was trying to get away, she was going to help him. She didn't care what Britt thought about that. She sent him a quick text:

B KNOWS. I HAVE STRONG LEAD ON C IN LAS VEGAS. AT HARRAH'S. HEADED THERE NOW. TURN AROUND AND JOIN ME.

There, it felt good to send that. Britt had enough control. She wasn't going to see him hurt the one man who could bring her pleasure.

She grabbed her other phone and called the Harrah's main number. She needed whoever was the head of the cleaning crew. She believed they had a little mole on their staff, if not an outright terrorist. She was sure they would want to take care of that.

SIXTY-NINE

Was there a moment for sure when you know it's over? Was that where Britt was? He sure wasn't going to quit fighting, but he had killed many of his allies and failed to kill those he specifically set out to kill.

He could feel himself losing blood. If he did not turn this around soon, he might have a death as ignominious as Alexander the Great's: alcohol poisoning.

The work the back-alley doctor did helped but at quite a price. He cried and thrashed as the man cleaned the wounds and then stitched his manhood up. They found a place to park out of sight enough to make it worth their while to go there, and Britt allowed himself an hour's nap. He awoke feeling a bit better, the pain meds kicking in a little, still painful, but with the edge off.

And then Naseem called; it felt like a call from a ghost. This was another miscalculation along with too many to count. He thought he knew what was in store. He could count on Red. She had her problems under control. He needed to kill Naseem, collect his prize, kill his nemesis, and pay someone who would fly when he said so.

Yes, this could still be salvaged. He dug the phone out and saw enough time had passed since Naseem called. He didn't want to make him think he was panicking. Even though that was a mild word for the thoughts running through his head.

He dialed the number. Naseem picked up.

"My boy. You decided to stay in the land of the living. How lucky you didn't follow orders, or you'd be dead. What came over you?" The words were difficult to muster. He felt weaker and weaker.

"I won't play your games, Britt. I won't even call you what you like to be called."

"Oh, I just did that Yankee thing for you. Seemed more properly spy if we were calling each other by stupid names." He laughed at his own joke.

"Where do we meet?"

"So you can try to kill me? What is this?"

"It's a challenge, Britt. A taunting. Nothing has gone right for you. Caitlin is alive. Grant Miller is alive. Because of *me*."

"Grant Miller is alive." He said this as if he already knew it, although it hit him like a punch in the gut.

"Your plan is an utter disaster," Naseem said. "A failure. All the people you targeted. They're alive. A brutal, utter disaster."

Britt sat unmoving and silent. His ears rang, whether from the truth or the blood, he didn't know. It didn't matter.

He debated whether to speak or not. He could leave the country right now; he was sure of it. But to leave it with his enemies intact? To be half a world away and not be able to solve a single problem? Death was better than that.

Maybe he was now ready for Naseem's silly games. "I'll be at the Heritage Air Strip in an hour. You can meet your beloved Allah there." He hung up, no longer sure if he was even close to the mark.

Seventy

The deadline hit. It was time. People stayed up just to see what happened. Live feeds showed a building in the middle of the night. Helicopters hovered in the dark, shining lights on the building to see if that was what Sabotage planned.

Britt smiled. This was his preferred outcome and definitely took his mind off all that went wrong. He made bets in every direction, but there had never been any doubt that if he could somehow get the American people to buy his worthless stock he would profit the most.

The trades were so minuscule and in so many names that it would never be possible to corral them all. In addition, much of the activity had already been captured and aggregated prior to actually getting to this moment, so everything else he raked from hard-earned money was truly just a bonus. What happened next was the real fun for him.

The website was off the charts. The hashtag #sabotage was

trending number one. He liked this. Britt uploaded the next sequence of code—so simple, so much doom.

Sabotage, the Clown, ambled back to the middle of the screen. He looked up and made a carnival gesture. A YouTube video appeared right above him. Sabotage appeared in the video, too. He looked left and right before unfurling his banner. It read:

HAVEN'T YOU HEARD OF SHORTING A STOCK?????

The video cut away. The Sabotage site stole one of the live feeds from a cable network. It showed the explosions on the roof of the building. Even if they found some of them, he knew there would be no way to find them all. It looked to him like they looked minimally. The explosions danced on the roof. They went off in random order, yet somehow looked choreographed. He loved it.

The anchors for the various networks started their hand-wringing. "Who was behind this?" they asked the audience. "Why would they want to cause such disruption?" They had nothing but questions to fill their broadcasts. Questions and speculations. They filled the airwaves with them.

Britt kept the Las Vegas police scanner on just to monitor the police's progress. He heard them call in the tip on Trump Towers. They would meet Britt Vasher pretty soon. They would have to work a little bit to get from there to who he really was.

But then he was wide-eyed. Was that what they said? He was sure he had heard it. They called him Britt Vance, not Britt Vasher. It wasn't rocket science putting these two things together, but it was still much quicker than he expected.

He set up Seth as the decoy to make them believe there was someone above him, and he was dead. It probably wouldn't last forever, he knew, but it would give him a head start.

How did they know his name?

He was afraid he knew.

SEVENTY-ONE

President Morgan, with his stellar approval ratings and his eye trained on history, nearly retched after the latest attacks. They were outrageous and wrong, but he realized there weren't really words strong enough for them.

For the first time in his nearly seven years in office, the president could honestly say he had no idea what to do—that terrified him. He knew he needed to speak to the people. He knew they were waiting on him. And now, when he was needed the most, he had the least to say. He asked Vanessa to set it up and said nothing else to her. He climbed back to the podium, looked into the cameras, and started to speak.

"Ladies and gentlemen, citizens in the United States of America, I'm coming to you tonight. It is different from any other moment that I've had with you. For a couple of reasons."

He looked out at the press corps and noticed just how different the mood was. These men and women were normally jaded, bored, barely following along. Now they were riveted.

"As you know, I generally have a large hand in writing my own speeches. That is important to me. But I still get some help, and I still use a teleprompter. I don't think that's any surprise, but it's true."

Even crusty old Marnie Teeter, always a critic, looked at him like he imagined the press had looked at Kennedy.

"But tonight, I'm not speaking with either a prepared speech or a teleprompter. I did the same thing this morning. Want to know why? Because I have no idea what to say. None."

He paused for emphasis.

"To anyone affected by today's attacks, nothing I can say will make it better. I love you, I feel for you, I want to help, but that's all meaningless to you right now. I know it."

Gazing straight into the camera, he spoke to the viewers.

"To those of you who sit in your homes now not knowing whether it's safe to come out, I understand that. And I don't know what to say to you. But I know this: we have to go on. We will go on. John Wayne said that courage was being scared to death but saddling up anyway. That's where we are. This is scary. But we ride, because that's who we are."

He sensed he was hitting the right notes. So he carried on.

"And for those who are responsible for this, whether it is one or one million, let me tell you: we will come at you with our best people—from Alabama to Boston and South Central, LA. You will see us coming. You will look us in the eye. You will pay for what you have done. We outnumber you. We will outsmart you. We will defeat you."

He hoped he believed these words. He thought he did. Then he caught himself. He still believed in America. He nodded and finished it up:

"We have grown used to prosperity and peace in this land. For most of our times, we were in a war as often as we were out of one. But now, we have come to expect peace. Expect freedom. This may make for some trying days ahead, but that's when we've always banded together and made our greatest strides. This will not defeat us. That is the one thing I can tell you tonight. This will not defeat us."

He released the podium and gave a nod. "Thank you."

The small audience stood and applauded. He did the impossible: after this awful day, he made people believe, which was almost more than he could say about himself.

SEVENTY-TWO

Tony was down. Flames licked the house. Sirens would soon pierce the air, and Pal Joey headed for the body.

He walked straight-up gangsta. This was his scene now.

Tony tried to crawl from the scene, scarred, burned, and whimpering. He edged toward his phone.

Joey got there first.

"What's this, bitch?" He held up the phone and clicked on the home screen. It was locked.

"Please," Tony managed.

"You fuckin tried to kill me today. Recognize me? It's Pal Joey."

Tony closed his eyes and made a sound.

The most pain-filled thing Joey had ever heard.

Joey took his $1,000 gator shoe and raked it across Tony's arm. A piece of flesh came off.

Tony screamed in a tone that made both of the other men

wince.

"No! No!"

"What's the code, bitch?"

"Please?"

Joey pulled his foot back up, bluffing, because he couldn't stand that sound again. It was not human.

Tony made a smaller version of it anyway, afraid of the pain that would follow.

"What's the motherfuckin' code?" Joey demanded.

"3383. Please."

Joey punched in the code. It worked. He nodded and gazed back up at the car. No sirens yet. He smiled. He had time.

He unzipped his pants, stood over to Tony, who started whimpering again, and pissed on him—full flow—on his back and face where the burns were. It would make Tony feel better. Tony stopped whimpering and was quiet. Joey turned and walked back to the limo.

On his way, he was almost sure he heard Tony thank him. Damn, it was bad to be that bitch.

Marvin started the car. Joey was about to get in when Tony's phone got a text from Red:

B KNOWS. I HAVE STRONG LEAD ON C IN LAS VEGAS. AT HARRAH'S. HEADED THERE NOW. TURN AROUND AND JOIN ME.

His luck had turned. This sounded promising. He got into the limo and told Marvin, "Take us to John Wayne Airport. It's the closest."

He looked at Raylon and said, "Call our boy and get us that helicopter back. We goin' to Vegas."

SEVENTY-THREE

Red sounded like a serious woman. It helped her many times in the past. She had the voice of a badass but professional bitch. She thanked her lucky stars that it was a fill-in working the human resources desk, and she imagined that the general panic of the day didn't hurt. The woman rolled over fast.

She knew she was dealing with Tonya Jamison. She told the fill-in she was wanted in connection with the terror attacks today; that she wasn't to speak to her or let her know anything about her coming.

"Tell me about Ms. Jamison," Red said. There was no room for questioning.

"Single. One child, a boy. She pays support on him. It's deducted."

"How old?"

The woman didn't stop to ask how this was germane in a terror attack. She did the math. "Six."

Red murmured approvingly. "Is there a name?"

"No, but …"

Red cut her off. "Thank you. Please ask Ms. Jamison to come to HR. Have her meet me there, and please do not tell her why I am there."

The fill-in said nothing.

Red said a stern thank you and ended the call.

Traffic was now lighter than usual, but it bunched up ahead. She hadn't heard from Tony. She hoped he was all right. The last block to Harrah's took forever.

Finally, the cabbie pulled up front. Red gave him a healthy tip from Steve's money, and she hurried inside. She also tipped him Steve's clothes in the back seat, although he didn't know it yet.

She nodded at the doormen and fished out the old and out-of-date FBI badge that had once been an incredible find. With some help from some of Vegas' most seedy characters, she turned this into her image—a really nice fake. She hoped she wouldn't have to do any more than flash it.

Luckily, fill-in wanted the terrorist out of his room. She grabbed Tonya roughly by the arm, said only "FBI," and headed to the small room they provided her.

Harrah's was helping nicely.

She threw Tonya in the chair and made sure the windowless door was locked.

"Ms. Jamison, I'm not with the FBI. That was bullshit." She pulled a long, thin knife out of her bag and moved it toward the woman.

"You probably will wish I were with the FBI. They have rules they have to live by." She sat on the table.

Tonya clearly knew what this was about.

"I hate rules. Don't you?" Red wanted to get this done, but

she took her time. She knew there was a cadence to this, a rhythm that yielded results.

"We have your son. I know you're a shitty mom because he's with his *fucking dad*, but even shitty moms generally love their kids and don't want to see them tortured and killed, right?"

Every bit of color drained from Tonya's face.

"Now, let's talk. I think you know why I'm here. I think you know exactly where my little party bitch is. I'm on a short time schedule. I need to know where, and you've got just enough time to start talking before I start cutting and making fucking phone calls."

She knew from Tonya's look this wasn't going to take long. To make things better, she heard the chirp of her cell phone. Tony texted her. He was on his way to Vegas. The night got better in just a few brief moments.

SEVENTY-FOUR

R ed wanted to be free of Britt. She depended on no one, but, when her father ran into a problem with embezzlement, she only knew one person who could loan her the quarter of a million dollars that would keep him out of jail. Since she hadn't been able to pay it off with the princely interest rate of twenty percent, she was still working it off little by little. Knowing what was at stake for Britt, she thought she knew how to make things right.

She called Britt. "I have a surprise for you."

"A good one?"

"A great one."

"What is it?"

"First, a question. If I could bring Caitlin to you alive, what would you make of it?"

"How quickly?"

"Within an hour."

Britt thought about this. This was his original plan after all, but Red wouldn't think anything about killing for him. Would he like to finish her off himself, or would he like to give her a shot at redemption?

See? There he was, talking all silly again. Caitlin couldn't be redeemed. She couldn't be brought back into line. That was for certain. But Red? She was another story. He knew she saw him for what he was but was less sure of what this meant to him. She was a woman who could be fierce and quiet at the same time. She was as cold-blooded as he. He could tell she admired him. Whether she liked him romantically seemed quite a jump.

He stopped himself. Why was he even talking about frivolous things at a time like this? He needed to be calm and collected and just worried about getting away.

"I don't know," he said coldly. "Capture her first, and then we'll talk."

Finally, he thought. He was thinking straight again. But, he admitted to himself, he really hoped she could pull this off.

SEVENTY-FIVE

R ed could tell Tonya was not going to be a problem. She handcuffed the maid with her bondage handcuffs and paraded her right in front of the employees, moving her arms so it looked like they were lesbian lovers in lockstep.

Tonya didn't make a sound.

Good girl, Red thought, *that would make it easier to kill her when the time came.*

Red led her to the end of the hall, checked to see that her audience left, and turned to the right. She threw Tonya onto the first elevator she could find, and she followed her to the right floor.

She saw Tonya's look many times before, the look of someone who was trying to decide whether she could or would make a move. Red punched her hard in the back.

Tonya's knees buckled.

"I can tell you're thinking bad luck thoughts, Tonya. I can get out my phone. Do you want me to get out my phone?" She wielded the phone like she would a knife, moving it in front of Tonya's face and smirking.

"No! I'm not thinking anything!"

Red smacked her across the face.

"That was for lying."

Red was taught that by an old mob boss years ago. She thought Tonya was lying, but she didn't know for sure. To hit her meant she could read her mind if she actually had those thoughts, and it made her think she was crazy if she hadn't thought them. Either response was helpful to Red.

"Let's not make that mistake again."

She saw the contorted look of utter fear on Tonya's face. It worked perfectly.

The elevator opened. They walked ahead.

She could tell Tonya was thinking. She stopped in front of the room.

Red gave her a death stare.

Tonya nodded at the right room.

Red signaled her to stay quiet.

Tonya was going to.

Red knocked on the door and then moved back so only Tonya would be seen.

The door opened—amateurs.

Red swung into motion, gun drawn, and then her jaw dropped. There were more people here than she expected. That was a very good thing.

SEVENTY-SIX

The body was wheeled into the third bay of the Las Vegas City Morgue. Both officers were there and arriving just in time from her embarrassing endeavor at the airport was Mandy LaPierre, with whatever dignity she could muster. She had risked a whole lot for Naseem and Grant, and she hoped her career didn't end up in a place like this. The smell, the cold, the clammy feeling the place gave her ... it was too much. She needed to get this over quickly and get on to something that didn't feel like death.

Nick had his money on homicide. It was theoretically made to look like a suicide, but this didn't seem like their killer's style. Had he been the set-up man, too important, or known too much to keep around? Was there someone even bigger leading the charge?

Gates thought it was a decoy.

Mandy had her mind elsewhere, still thinking about Grant

and Naseem and what was yet to happen. At some point, she was going to have to go to someone over her head and at least give her suspicions about the possibility of a frame-up. But she wanted to give them a chance to find out what Caitlin knew and make this whole career-risk worth her time. She hadn't eaten all day and couldn't imagine eating now. She was scared. She had a feeling she was wasting her time here. She was sure some of the higher-ups were suspicious about her charges' escape.

The doctor began the dictation, and everyone hushed. "My name is Dr. Charu Rahima. I am in charge of this forensic exam. As we begin, I would like to ask each person in the room to state their name and credentials."

Nick just started giving his details when they heard the sound. It was a dull whirring coming from the table. He thought it was possibly a tool warming up until he saw the look on Mandy's face. This was not normal.

Mandy yelled, "Get out of the way," but it was too late. The flesh-covered bomb exploded, flashing brilliantly and sending a whole new style of medical shrapnel flying far down hallways and high above them. It didn't matter. By the time those objects landed, they were all already dead.

SEVENTY-SEVEN

Red got everyone in the room. She couldn't believe her luck, and she was so surprised she nearly didn't react well. It was clear Grant was going for a piece, but she released Tonya and made her intentions clear. Grant smartly backed off.

Oh, this was rich. She would tell Britt she owed him nothing further. She could tell him to go to hell. And for once, he would have to listen.

She motioned for them to sit on the floor.

They did without a whimper.

She grabbed her phone out of the bag and dialed Britt.

He answered after one ring.

"Britt, if I had another enemy in the room as well as your piece of ass, we'd call the deal with my dad even, right? I mean, I've covered my end."

Britt was silent. Miller was there. He could still hope.

"Who?"

"Well, your golden boy. Thought dead. Grant? Miller?"

He was speechless for a long time. Red finally felt the need to speak. "They're both here. Caitlin and Grrrrannnt. With me. That would take care of it, right?"

"Yes, indeed, but ..." He was really rattled. That was a first.

"Well, I'm gonna send you a picture in a minute. You need to get here. It's going to have your bitch and Caitlin in it. Ha! Get it? And it's going to have a dead Mexican-looking chick in it. Because I need them to understand that I mean business."

With that, she shut off her phone. She smiled, reached in her bag, and screwed on a silencer. She aimed the gun at Tonya's head and perkily said, "Say cheese!"

SEVENTY-EIGHT

Britt had a very short window of time to make his decision. He could walk away, having made a thousand men's fortunes, and live with relative safety and security. He didn't need to run any more of the Sabotage protocols.

He could quit while he was ahead—quit while he was alive. He had been paying off people around the world for five years. Now, he had the money to do it for five hundred more.

But he had failed on such a basic level—all of the most important people in his strategy still walked and breathed. Grant could outlive him—could he ride away knowing that his enemy and his lover would most likely be reunited?

This would not be a win. This would be torture knowing that his enemies frolicked while he was away from the action.

He asked the driver to take him to the airstrip. It was the dumbest thing he could do and the only one that could make him smart again.

SEVENTY-NINE

Joey now controlled the phone, the code, and the luxury of the entire texting history between Tony and Red. First off, this bitch was *fine*. She had sent Tony two pictures, but they were enough. Long legs, nice, real titties, and a real hand-spanked white-girl ass. She looked good—real good. Joey was embarrassed he was thinking of a thing like pussy at a time like this, but he was. Even with a helicopter, it was a long ride to Vegas.

Joey was corresponding with her, almost exclusively using Tony's own words, copying things he said, changing them slightly, sending them to her. He told her he was on his way and then tried to make sure she told him where to meet in a way he could fully find without using too much shorthand.

She told him she had new hostages she could use in negotiating with "B." "B" was obviously the mastermind or close to the top. It seemed as though "B" hadn't cleaned up his mess. This couldn't be better if Joey were writing the script.

Where should we meet?

Meet us at the Heritage Air Strip.

Tony would know. Joey responded with a simple, *K.* He had enough time to google that shit. Then he could meet his new friend in person.

EIGHTY

Being in a near-death experience like Grant experienced in September 11 and then again today, changes you in a couple of ways. First, you appreciate and cherish life more, and, second, you feel like you've already cheated death once, so why not again?

Grant now stood with the woman he loved seven feet away from a cold-blooded killer who had just killed Caitlin's savior and looked ready to kill them. He realized this was his chance ... to make up for the embarrassment he caused Caitlin, to make up for the embarrassment he caused everyone. Not everyone got a second chance, but he firmly believed this was his.

He was uncuffed. He was bigger than the woman. If he lost, he cheated death by a few hours or a few years, depending on how you looked at it, and he would save his dear Caitlin, because he was taking out the other woman, no matter what.

He didn't look at his lover or do any of the trite things that end up getting you detected. He waited until the moment she tried to take the picture of her catch, the dumbest thing she could possibly do.

Then, without giving anyone notice, he launched himself. One step and then a push off. Red realized it—too late. She tried to rearrange her focus, but he was already on top of her. His intent was to push her hard into the mirrored closet and then drive her into the floor. She got her hand onto the trigger and fired again, but the bullet went into the ceiling. She was semi-unconscious on the floor.

Grant grabbed the gun and motioned for Caitlin. She followed him, no questions needed. They ran down the hallway, needing a plan.

EIGHTY-ONE

Naseem had time to get to the airstrip. He texted Grant where he was heading, having no desire to have Grant follow him and somehow foul things up. He already knew his plan would work; why not let him be there?

On the way, he stopped at an apartment where he had stayed and still had a lease. He peered around the corner, making sure no one was there. It hadn't made it into the police's hands yet, he guessed. He found the key taped under the step, just where he left it, and went inside.

He turned on the lights and looked at the picture of his parents on the counter. They were all he really left. Then he picked up the sweet heft of the Quran. He thumbed its rice-thin pages. He wished he still believed his promises. He didn't know anymore.

But he believed in his new mission. It was clear and easy to understand—just get close, and it would be over.

He went to the closet and stood on his tip-toes. All the way in back, he found the vest. Bulky, heavy, but accurate and perfect for his mission. It took him a second to find the detonator, but it wasn't far away.

He took off his shirt and put on the vest. It was too tight, but he made do. He would be thinner very soon. He grabbed a jacket, which would better hide what he was wearing. Vegas nights got cool enough, and the jacket wouldn't look or feel out of place. He put the detonator back in the jacket pocket. He would put in the batteries when he arrived at Heritage.

He had come full-circle in the last day. He was still going to be a martyr—only for a different cause: his.

EIGHTY-TWO

Grant and Caitlin grabbed a cab in front of Harrah's. Anywhere else, with Grant's broken face and the harrowed look that Caitlin was wearing, they would have looked like the craziest people on the planet; in Vegas, they stood out but barely.

As they sat down, Grant's phone went off. He looked down and, to his surprise, saw that Naseem texted him:

HERITAGE AIR STRIP. HEADED THERE.

He was glad Naseem had reached out but very wary. Why would the man who ditched him care if he knew where this was going down?

Grant ran with two thoughts. One was that it was a decoy. The second was probably closer to being right.

He looked down at his phone and punched in a number. He told the driver to head to Heritage.

Caitlin was in shock. She mourned the loss of her friend, who died because of her. She had seen lots in her time but not this. She was trying to fight the effects of shock to see if she needed to help her man. After the display in the hotel room, she hoped he would still have her.

The operator finally answered. "White House Switchboard."

"My name is Agent Grant Miller. I need to speak to the president."

He could tell that the woman didn't know whether to treat him seriously or not.

"Sir …"

"Go ask the people around him. He will want to talk to me."

He held for about two minutes. Then he heard that unmistakable voice.

"What the hell do you want?" There was no warmth this time. "I have given you every rope I can find and you keep hanging yourself."

"Sir, I have done nothing of the sort. Mandy was in on the action taken on the plane. You can get that from her now."

"I'd like to if she weren't dead," the president said. "She was blown up by one of your boys, best I can tell."

This hit Grant hard. He didn't know how to respond.

"Sir, I guess we'll have to take this up tomorrow. Right now, I have a lead on the terrorist. You're right about one thing: he once was one of ours."

"Why are you calling me? Don't you just act on your own?"

Grant knew he had to ignore this. "Sir, we're headed to Heritage Air Strip. I don't know if Britt is there or not, but we don't need to spook him. We need our best people in place. I also need a tranquilizer gun."

"A WHAT?" the president said loud enough for everyone in the room to jump.

"You heard me. Loaded for large game. Something like that."

"What do you …?"

"I am sure this is not protocol, Mr. President, but I'm not far from the grounds, and I need to discontinue any communication. You have extended me every courtesy, and I believe when you have reviewed everything, you will know that I have acted in a trustworthy manner. I only ask this one last favor."

Then Grant Miller hung up on the president of the USA.

EIGHTY-THREE

Britt was waiting, woozy, wounded, and ready to see this play out. He saw Caitlin and Grant come. He saw them get out at the perimeter, and then he saw them split up. He expected everything but this. He saw Grant walk straight toward him. He could no longer see Caitlin.

Grant walked directly toward his limo. Britt stepped out. He called for some personal security. Only in Vegas could you find such a thing in the middle of the night. This was amateur hour, but they would do.

The sight of Grant hit Britt hard. He was still reeling from his injuries, and this man was the symbol of how something that started so right still seemed hollow.

"How many are coming?" He smiled to show he expected the play. He didn't know if it was convincing.

"You don't need to know. You never could count anyway."

"I've ruined your last several years, Grant Miller. You don't need to insult my intelligence."

"And here I thought I ruined everything all by myself."

"Where did that exquisite piece of ass go?"

"I'll tell you that as soon as you surrender."

Britt laughed.

"You know what? I wasn't on the wrong side when you busted me. You know that whole thing, right?" There was something in his eyes—part anger, part curiosity, still interested in what his rival thought of him even after all that went wrong. "Those men were national security risks. The worst kind of rogues."

"There were ways to handle that. You knew that. You gave me no choice."

Grant looked back at Britt. This whole line of questioning stung him for a second. He took himself back there, thought it through.

"You might have thought that then. You might even be right, but you haven't been on the right side for a long time,"

"Right and wrong. We both lost the meaning of those words a long time ago."

"Don't try to equate me with you," Grant tried to think of harsher words, but nothing seemed to fit the evil of what this man did. Was it really all because of him?

"I fucked your woman." Britt said it with a grin.

Grant didn't know what to say to that. He was so tired.

"Yes, you did." He watched Britt intensely. He seemed nervous and out of place, much worse than when he first told him about the charges against him so many years ago.

Grant continued his study of Britt and spotted something he hadn't expected—a drop of blood ... then another. It fell just between Britt's legs.

"Somebody hit you?"

Britt aimed his pistol and shot at Grant. He moved his aim like he was playing a weird game of Russian Roulette. One bullet skittered across the floor. One went wide. And one hit Grant in the shoulder as he tried to roll out of the way.

"Where is she?" He screamed at Grant. He was going to regain control. "She's leaving with me." He fired again wildly.

Grant writhed in pain and couldn't formulate an answer. He thought for a moment the wound was worse than it was. Then he was trying to gather his thoughts and stall Britt for as long as possible. Britt put a new clip in his gun. Grant heard him change the clip, heard the metallic noise as he waited for the sound of more thunderous gunshots. He thought he could stall him if he could answer.

"She's coming … with the other friend you tried to kill."

EIGHTY-FOUR

They met the agent a mile away from the airstrip. Grant flashed his headlights as he crossed the parking lot, and the nameless man returned the gesture. Grant pulled next to him and both windows rolled down. The agent handed Grant a package containing syringes and sedatives.

"Boss said you'll like these better than a tranq gun. Easier to hide and you can measure the dose."

"Boss next time needs to listen to what he's asked to do," snipped Grant.

"I'll tell her that. Does that mean you don't want these handguns I was told to bring you?"

Grant took them without saying a word.

He stopped the car before leaving the lot. "Now, I've got to figure this out."

Grant hadn't done anything like this in years, but he managed to carefully fill the syringe. He put the cap back on it and handed it to Caitlin. Then he gave her a backup, using the same procedures, before he left. He handed the materials and one of the handguns to Caitlin. He gave her his thoughts on how Naseem would most likely enter. He could scan the area and see where anyone trained would try to join the scene.

The wind still felt hot even this late. Caitlin waited, every sense heightened even though she found herself so drained from the insanity of the day. Waiting is always difficult; this was torture.

Finally, she saw a black Chevy Suburban, what she was looking for. Just as Grant asked her to, she flagged him down.

This surprised Naseem. He saw Caitlin's picture before, although he had never met her. She still managed to maintain an air of beauty around her even with all that happened that day. She was tired, but he knew immediately who she was. He expected to beat them to the airstrip, and he wondered if there were any other surprises.

He nodded at Caitlin as he rolled down the window. Pleasantries seemed completely unnecessary.

"What's wrong?"

"Grant's in there with Britt. He told me to give you the lay of the land before going in there."

"Okay, what's up?"

This was going according to the plan Grant gave her. She now opened the door without asking and slid in the passenger side.

"Start driving. Slowly."

Naseem had no choice but to obey her.

"He can't stop me."

"He doesn't want to. He just wants to aid you in doing it right."

Naseem was surprised by this as well. This was all too easy. He eased the SUV into the hangar. He could see Grant and Britt on

260

the other end.

Then she heard those terrible shots. She didn't know who had fired, but she realized what she had to do regardless. The second Naseem looked in the direction of the shots was all she needed.

Only at the last minute did he see her jab the syringe in his neck. He instinctively reached for his pocket, where he had the detonator. But his head hit the horn before that could happen.

Caitlin jammed the car into park from the passenger side and emerged, having unknowingly made herself a sitting duck.

EIGHTY-FIVE

It wasn't supposed to happen like this. She was supposed to let Naseem get much closer and then knock him out. Now she was at the other end, and Grant could clearly see it was her. Naseem was their best chance for a Mexican standoff; now he had nothing, and he was outdrawn by the riffraff.

Grant mouthed, "I love you," as she approached. He wasn't sure she could even see it. He wondered if this was where he was going to lose her, so soon after finding her again.

At that moment, a helicopter began descending out of the sky—Britt's ride to a place he and Caitlin could seek medical help and then make love for ages on the beach. He could be so magnanimous now. It was almost like it was supposed to be. He motioned to two of the guards to grab Miller. He knew he would play the bluff now that others were watching him. And if they were, he knew they would have already moved in.

"I'll let you watch us leave," Britt said, as if he were granting the man a pardon. He could text the men once they got off the ground and have Miller tortured and left for dead. Local help like these guys always liked that.

He took Caitlin by the arm. She started to struggle, but she looked at Grant, who was telling her no. He couldn't do anything to help her. They moved out of the hangar and toward the helicopter, now just a few feet off the ground.

Britt handed Caitlin to one of his men. "Wait here," he said, with a loving expression of a sixteen year-old in love. "I'll go clear us space."

Britt walked up to the door of the helicopter, gun drawn, pointed at Caitlin, urging her to come quicker to him.

He didn't expect the Air Jordan of Pal Joey to land right in his face.

EIGHTY-SIX

Joey used the surprise and the leverage he had on the man. He climbed down and pounced on him, landing hard right into Britt's jaw, which Britt was clearly not prepared for. He now had the man who tried to kill him pinned to the ground, groggy, and with a pained and helpless look on his face. He had a knee on each of Britt's forearms, and he punched him in the face—hard—once again to make him stay down. He could feel Britt's teeth sting his knuckles. He knew he hit him good.

The whirring of the helicopter blades was subsiding. The rent-a-thugs were paralyzed, not wanting to do anything that might jeopardize their bouncer gigs at the local strip clubs. Everyone inched slowly to the action, but no one really knew why they were doing this.

Joey reached in his back pocket and pulled out a Glock pistol. He had only used it once on a person almost five years ago in San Diego. With all he spewed in his rap, he didn't like that, really. But he was going to like this.

He took the gun and put it in Britt's mouth.

The cops were coming. He could see their America-colored lights closing in on the scene. They would love nothing more than to waste him as well as Britt. Joey knew this. He was prepared for this.

Raylon climbed down from the copter and was pleading with him to stand down. "We got this nigga. Let go."

But this was personal. This was his moment. After the image he cultivated, how could he just let this bitch go? This baby killer? This terrorist? Naw, man. Shit was real. And he was gonna watch him squirm and then watch him die just like Johnny Cash, or Willie Nelson, or whoever the fuck that was.

But then he had a picture. He could hear the cops approaching, weapons drawn. He could hear their high-pitched shouts, their boots echoing against the floor of the hangar. And then he had a thought—of his Dago homies on lockdown, the unlucky ones, the hard cases who hadn't made it. He pictured them. He pictured them interacting with this bitch, letting them have their day, letting them be patriotic.

There was at least one more helicopter overhead. In the dark, he couldn't tell if it was media or police. He saw one brave black man, probably an airport employee, maybe the only one who knew who he was, videotaping the whole thing with his cell phone. He made a gesture to him to come closer.

He put down the gun. Sent it flying along the ground well out of Britt's reach. He put his hands up to show the cops he was no longer strapped. He beckoned again for his close-up. When the man got close enough, he turned to the camera and sang, loudly,

"Bad-ass straight up from Dago,

I'm the baddest pimp in the cell,

Feeding down punk-ass bitches
To all of my brothas in jail."

He laughed loudly. So did the man holding the camera. He flashed his signs. That would be a hit so big Elvis would be looking up at his ass. He would find a way to rhyme "FBI" with "fucking high." Pal Joey was about to really blow up. He was back from the dead.

He waited for the cops to approach and to secure this bitch. They did. Then he stood up and walked away, the newest American hero.

EPILOGUE

LEAVENWORTH

In real life, there is no grand escape. There are rarely D.B. Coopers who extend beyond their crimes into the ether. Britt now knew this. The Bond villain in real life has an inmate number and eats the same starchy, bland prison food endured by the embezzler and the child molester.

He liked how they treated him with utter fear for their safety. They required half a dozen men to transport him anywhere, and then they left him alone, as they were afraid he would be killed by any other lifer trying to gain status for himself.

He wished the rapper would have killed him then and there. That would have given him immortal status, if only in a strange way. He could have lived on in the minds of America, pictured next to his creation, who unfortunately died with him. His design required him to sign off on each additional attack, so, while the damage he did was widespread and incredibly costly, it stopped when he was unable to key in the sequence for the next attacks. People reacted strangely to this, almost not knowing how to not be afraid anymore.

He had not done this out of some altruistic vein. He merely wanted to control every aspect of this operation and couldn't imagine a Bond villain not setting the attacks himself.

When they finally figured out where the server was hidden, and, after the first technician died from tripping a booby trap he set, they were able to see what else he planned. Facebook and Twitter were spared much damage, and this puzzled many people. But he needed those networks to quickly spread the messages. The computer techs figured out that the code that would have infested them and sent them into decline if not outright death was two days away, the final act of the maddest man there had ever been. The code was exquisite, and more than one of the people who knew what they were looking at secretly saluted this man. That was something you couldn't say out loud, but it was surely there.

The government was preparing its case against Britt, scheduled to start just five days short of a year after the attack, when one of the planning guards forgot to check a rarely-used vestibule on the prison's main floor on Britt's path to the courthouse. One of the prisoners housed on the same lock-down as Britt, who actually was friendly with him, jumped out with a pristinely made shiv and slashed Britt's throat. He also did a pretty mean job opening up his right wrist. The man, Victor Stillings, dropped the knife immediately and surrendered. He had already memorized the codes and all the directions to the bank accounts Britt told him held millions for him and his family.

Britt smiled as he bled to death on the prison floor. He made the only escape he could, the only one left.

LONDON, ENGLAND

Naseem's picture still appeared on the occasional television show, but Grant made good on his promise to make things as easy as he possibly could. The story got much more play in the States, and, after Grant arranged, with some help from above, a flight to Bermuda and then a boat to England, things cooled off.

Naseem grew a beard, stayed out of the sun, and looked less and less like the angry man that stared out of his last passport picture, the one the press loved to show.

He paid for his crimes every day in the never-ending sense of dread he felt when anything out of the ordinary happened. This would be his own private, minimum-security prison for years to come. He knew it wasn't enough for many people, and, in fact, he questioned whether it was enough penance for him, but he wasn't looking to heap anything else on himself, at least right now. He would blend in and eventually slip into a more Mediterranean country, where he hoped to disappear into normalcy.

Grant sent him some money. It helped. Grant knew he could have been killed, and Naseem spared him. He wasn't going to write him a love song, but he wasn't going to forget him either. That to him was the greatest trait of Americans: remembering the good much longer than the bad.

He questioned everything now: Allah, America, England, life. But at least he was alive to ask those questions.

LOS ANGELES

"Terrorista" by Pal Joey, with a rare co-writer credit to his friend Raylon, turned out to be the biggest hit of the year. It was a dope track and was remixed by everyone. Pal Joey appeared simultaneously on the covers of *Rolling Stone, Vibe* and *Time*, a feat no one else could claim. His back catalogue was selling and being licensed at a pace that made Jay-Z envious.

Some rappers and others in the community thought he should have pulled the trigger and called him out for it, considering how many of Joey's own people were killed, but they were most likely just jealous of the success. Raylon told him to quit listening. He knew he did the right thing.

He met and had taken pictures with Grant and Caitlin a couple of times, but there were no reunions planned. If he hadn't found the phone, none of this would have happened. He knew he was the true hero. He was the only rapper who showed up high to the White House and could add a Presidential Medal to his bling. And he didn't care who bitched about it.

JEKYLL ISLAND, GA

In the latter parts of the 19th century and the first decade or two of the 1900s, most of the world's elite wintered on Jekyll Island— the Rockefellers, Vanderbilts, Morgans, Pulitzers, and others. This was where the Federal Reserve was designed in 1913.

The millionaires built what they called cottages but were really mini-mansions. They were positioned close to each other and close to the beautiful club that was built to house all of those egos.

The church there was no less special, built in the same style, and featured stained glass windows by Louis Comfort Tiffany himself. The piece, one of only five in the world, featured an angel looking down on the scene below. It was the true work of a master, seeming more like a translucent painting than a piece of glass. It seemed to Grant like the perfect place to have a wedding.

He and Caitlin stood in front of that angel as they said their vows. Only their families, his slightly bigger than hers, were allowed to come. They kept it an absolute secret, and, judging from the lack of photographers outside, they succeeded in giving the paparazzi the slip.

They came outside as husband and wife, completing a circle begun years earlier. Caitlin seemed satisfied and calm. He felt happy and fulfilled.

He hoped they could make it through the next couple of days unnoticed. They brought beach disguises. After years of the Playboy Mansion and late nights in the club, he knew he left that behind. Nothing compared with this woman, and he would risk anything to keep that true. All he needed was an evening with dragonflies and a night on the beach. Anything else was a bonus.

ACKNOWLEDGEMENTS

I am forever indebted to my great friend Liz Giordano, who pushed me to seek an audience for *Sabotage*. She has been an editor, a cheerleader, and a willing helper in advocating for this book.

As of this date, several of my friends have read *Sabotage:* Bill McCullah, Lisa Haglund, Amy Lamphere, Susan Kelly, Amber Hruska, Cecelia Havens, Beth Rich, Jess Meadows, and Julie Gibson. Their suggestions were pivotal to seeing my way to the final manuscript. Thank you to all of you!

And finally, to my agent, Italia Gandolfo, for making this process so smooth and fun. You are the best!

ABOUT THE AUTHOR

Dale Wiley has had a character named after him on CSI, owned a record label, been interviewed by Bob Edwards on NPR's Morning Edition and made motorcycles for Merle Haggard and John Paul DeJoria. He has three awesome kids and spends his days working as a lawyer fighting the big banks. Dale is the author of the bestselling novel, *The Intern*.

Check Dale's site at http://www.dalewiley.com/ for updates and details.

Preview *The Intern*—a political action thriller by Dale Wiley.

It's 1995, and life is great for Washington, DC intern Trent Norris. But life can change in a moment--and does when Trent becomes the prime suspect in two murders and a slew of other crimes. Overnight, he becomes the most wanted man in America. Trent has to find a way—any way—out. He holes up at The Watergate on a senator's dime and enlists a call girl as his unwitting ally. But with the media eating Trent alive, he doesn't have long before they catch him. From the tony clubs of Georgetown to murders on Capitol Hill, The Intern has all the twists and turns of a classic DC thriller, with an added comedic flair.

CHASING MURDERERS,
HOOKERS, AND
SENATORS
ACROSS DC
WASN'T IN THE
JOB DESCRIPTION

"The Intern is smart, funny, and tough . . . one of the best mysteries I've read."
—Kinky Friedman, Governor of the Heart of Texas

THE
INTERN
DALE WILEY

PROLOGUE

"Are you going to kill me?"

Worry lines deepened into furrows as he stared at the short, silver barrel pointed at his forehead. When I didn't respond, he struggled to break free from the handcuffs chaining him to the bed.

I shifted my weight from one foot to the other, and he froze. His eyes darted around the room, and his mouth opened.

Waving the gun, I regained his attention. "I wouldn't if I were you."

He blanched until the color of his face matched the white hair on his head, and beads of sweat popped out on his brow.

To be perfectly honest, he could have yelled his head off and no one would have come. Fancy hotels, with rooms the size of a bus depot, thick yellow drapes and deep pile carpet designed to suck every sound out of the air, along with the constant air conditioning hum, ensured cries of passion or lover's quarrels went unheard.

And since he thought I was a killer, he wasn't going to scream. He didn't have to know there were no bullets in the gun. After all my misadventures, I didn't carry a loaded gun when killing wasn't on the menu.

I didn't like pointing a gun at anyone, even an empty one. It didn't make me feel strong. It didn't give me a rush of power. It almost reinforced the futility of my position. But I wanted the illusion of power. He needed to be still and listen to me.

Because I needed his help.

I let him squirm for a moment, the trembling of his lips getting lost in the scruff of his beard, before I shook my head.

He breathed long and slow, easing down from panic into fear. After checking the wrist shackled behind him by the tight-clamped cuffs, he looked at me, eyes wide, trying for sympathy, and asked, "Then, why am I here? What do you want?"

Relief shuddered through me. The question I had been waiting for.

"That's simple," I said. I set the gun on the dresser and leaned against it. My eyes bore into his. "I want to tell you my story."

CHAPTER
ONE

Almost everything in Washington was big and gray and ugly. I'm talking about the buildings, but a good number of the residents would also fall into the same category. The architects made everything look Roman and Greek, which might be all right if you were in Rome or Athens, but in DC the main part of the city looked like a bunch of poorly decorated wedding cakes.

The tourists, the players, and the street people, all converged uneasily every morning as I walked from my apartment on Capitol Hill to the Eastern Market Metro station. We all descended together beneath the Washington cement, waited impatiently for the next train, grabbed smooth steel bars, and held on as we rocketed in plastic cars through the belly of the town toward our jobs—to turn the wheels of bureaucracy in the most powerful city in the world. Some of the people clutched their seats and stared angrily, but most looked more like robots, reading the morning paper as they rumbled and shook toward another in a long line of work days. They were important people, the kind mothers and uncles in Poughkeepsie and Omaha and Boca Raton bragged on like crazy.

And I wasn't one of them. Well, not exactly. I worked for the government, but I had no desire to climb the DC ladder. To the contrary, I had already begun to plot my escape. To get away from the traffic, the lines, and the endless stream of silly, boring people: Capitol Hill pages slouching in ill-fitting department store suits; straw-haired society types covered in beige blouses and adorned with pearls; scowling, powerful white men who scared me for no good reason. I paid ungodly money for my half of an apartment, smaller than some closets, and thanks to my location in one of the city's "developing" neighborhoods, my car got broken into almost daily. I was tired of all that. I was tired of parking tickets. I was tired of humidity. I was tired of DC.

I worked for the NEA. No, not the education one—the artsy, standard-bearer of the Apocalypse, dirty-minded, potty-mouthed, slightly fruity one. A lightning rod to the closed-minded and a place for lovers of the perverse, the National Endowment for the Arts was different than most work places in DC—or so I thought.

I had worked at the Endowment for almost two months, and I wouldn't have been so excited to take the internship had I known how depressingly normal it was to work there. Despite all the rhetoric and name-calling, there were no Roman baths, no noon-time orgies, not even a poorly covered nipple.

But there were some advantages. The dress code wasn't as stringent as on Capitol Hill, so I got to wear jeans. Most of the people I encountered were smart, cool, funny, interesting, and enjoyed what they were doing. Maybe it wasn't quite like other places in Washington, but it was a lot more like them than most people thought.

When I walked through the door, I expected everyone to be in grant panel mode. Hundreds of grant applications, which had been handled with such care by those who had written them, would be scrutinized by a dozen or so arts professionals. Panel mode meant a great deal of running around and shouting, but there were clusters of people talking quietly, which was somehow unsettling.

The head mofo in charge in our office, Joe, calmly talked to Kurt, the office manager. Joe, with his beard, barrel chest, and brassy baritone voice, reminded me of a young, svelte, Jewish Santa Claus. Kurt was young, blond, extremely handsome, and extremely gay, the kind of guy women spend their whole lives wanting to convert. He was always full of expensive coffee and owned a taste in clothes I envied greatly.

"Just the man we're looking for," said Kurt, motioning me to follow him and Joe.

We walked around the maze of dividers, the tiny cubbyholes of bureaucracy, toward Joe's office, past a stack of used copy paper which was supposed to be recycled weeks ago. Joe had the only divider with a door, a sign of his status, and it was my favorite office, with lots of great posters and buttons and pictures of him when he was working in the theater. He sat down and shook his head, and I wondered what I could've possibly done.

"This thing is becoming such a headache." He spat the word "thing" out.

When Kurt both nodded and shook his head, almost at the same time, I was willing to bet Joe was talking about all the furor surrounding Regionarts.

"The Chairman told me before she left for the art mecca known as Las Vegas we are still supporting the program." The sarcasm dripped off Joe's tongue. "I don't think anyone believes it."

The Chairman reminded me of a mother-in-law in a TV sitcom: she was over fifty, wore long dresses she thought were hip, and had pretty brown hair, but if she were carrying a large purse, I would've been very afraid of her. The reason for Vegas? She had vowed to visit arts institutions in all fifty states during her reign—nice work if you can get it.

"We're supposed to have a teleconference next week, and we need you to gather all of the information on the project up to this point, make some sort of outline, send it to everyone involved, and set up the conference call."

To be put in charge of hand-holding and conference calling actually sounded halfway interesting; it was better than stacking and filing, anyway. Regionarts was a good program that gave gobs of money to regional groups who divided it among lesser-known artists. Some of the artists did really bizarre things with their money—like decorating a gallery space with used condoms—and "bizarre" was not our Chairman's favorite word.

"Want me to start now?"

Joe shook his head. "Nah. Go in and listen to some of the panel. You know most of the stuff, so it won't take too long."

I nodded and headed out of Joe's office and down the hall toward the panel room.

The actual granting took place in the panel, where someone's year of hard work was determined in a matter of minutes. Creative arts types mixed with those who handled the business side of things for the panel makeup. I had worked a couple of panels earlier, easy work from an intern's point of view—I sat and listened—but it was still rather nerve-wracking because people's livelihoods depended on what we were doing.

Walking into the room, I knew immediately who the artists were—the steel-sculpted black man with the blond dreadlocks, the Indian woman wearing a large scarf and larger glasses, poring over her grants book, and the robust black man in native African dress with a fatherly expression. The tables were arranged in a rectangle with everyone facing the middle. I took a seat on a corner, next to the tape recorder absorbing all of the madness, and smiled at the woman sitting next to me.

Pretty, conservatively dressed in a tweed blazer and a pair of jeans, she could have been twenty-five or forty. I couldn't make up my mind whether she would be overly serious or not.

Glancing down at the table, I caught a glimpse of the nameplate I'd made the day before. "Hi, Ann."

"Hi," she said, "You're …?"

"Trent, I work here." I never told anyone my intern status unless I had to. "How was your trip?"

Her lip curled. "Crowded. I hate flying NationAir because it's so cheap," she said. "But I love the hotel."

I had booked the flight but had nothing to do with the hotel. She didn't need to know either thing.

From reading the panelist biographies sitting in front of everyone, I learned she hailed from Nebraska. So I started a conversation about the Midwest, which eventually worked around to Midwestern punk bands like The Replacements and Husker Du, and I had a friend for the panel. Nothing is more important in Washington than having someone you can write notes to.

As the panel was called to order, I grabbed the pad of paper in front of me and uncapped the ballpoint pen—I had set the paper and pens out when setting up the room. I scribbled the first note and slid the page toward Ann.

Who is your favorite Charlie's Angel?

Her eyes met mine and she smirked. She replied and slid the page back.

Kate Jackson. Duh.

While Nancy Cho, the young Asian panel chair, went through the panel ground rules, Ann went straight for the juicy meat.

Any truth to the rumors about the torrid affair over in Education?

I struggled to keep a laugh from breaking out. It wasn't the free-wheeling Arts department providing the best gossip of the moment, but the snobby, reserved, and conservative Education department. I scribbled a response with glee.

The scuttlebutt is they were caught going at it in the mail room last week during lunchtime.

Neither of us were green enough to commit names to paper.

The panel reviewed applications for dance organizations to find those who were both interesting and financially stable.

Nancy dragged the stack of applications directly in front her. "Do we have consensus of what the panel is looking for?"

One member practically banged the table. "Financial stability."

The person to their left nodded. "No one should be granted money unless they are stable."

Rather ironic for them to want the applicants to be financially stable when they were asking for money.

Ann leaned forward. "We tend to give most of the money to the bigger organizations. I'd like to see the smaller groups benefit for a change."

The comments became a free-for-all.

"We need more cutting edge. The avant-garde."

"Ballet, for goodness sake. Can we focus on more traditional dance for once?"

The mustachioed agent across the table interjected nonsensical statements. "Dance ... creative expression ... freedom of movement." He waved his hands in the air.

Nancy checked her watch. "Let's get started, shall we?" She grabbed the first file off the top of the stack and read from the application.

As the morning wore on, I sat and listened, learning what got some people lots of extra money and got others shit-canned. Nancy checked her watch with increasing frequency and read the applications faster and faster, cutting short the discussion after each one with a call for decision.

Interesting.

Ann's face turned red when Nancy cut her off in the middle of yet another comment. She wrote furiously on her tablet and slid it across to me.

Gina Parks, the current dance flavor of the month, is performing tonight.

Understanding dawned. Nancy had been an amazing dancer before becoming badly injured. She rocketed through the grants—without giving them enough consideration—in hopes she could somehow make it to Gina's performance. Highly unlikely, unless she could convince the group to decide the applications by the rock-paper-scissors method.

Nancy grabbed the next application and read through it, her granny glasses sliding to the end of her nose. "I don't think we need to take the time for discussion on this. All in favor of passing?"

A woman across the table stood with such force, her chair nearly toppled. She planted her hands on the table and leaned toward Nancy. "That's enough. I am not going to stand by and watch as you rush your way through the application process."

Nancy looked like a snake just up and bit her, and a tendril of hair escaped her tight bun.

The woman took advantage of Nancy's moment of surprise. "The applications we are reviewing took months, sometimes nearly a year, to prepare, and we are obligated as the panel to give *each and every one* due consideration." Red spots appeared on her cheeks. "These are not simply words written on the form, but the culmination of hopes and dreams, and I refuse to crush anyone's dreams lightly."

James Rogers, the large man in traditional African dress, stood up and clapped his hands. "All right," he boomed. "Everyone out in the hall."

That was not what I expected.

His words were not a suggestion. I followed James, and Ann came out a moment later. Three other panelists walked dutifully out into the hall. What was going on?

"Make a circle," James said, a hint of a smile on his face.

We did.

James then led us through half an hour's worth of African tribal dances: moves to honor the sun and moves to honor the parents. Some looked like yoga, others more closely resembled modern dance. These were the first dance steps other than the box step I had ever attempted, and although some of the others picked up quicker, I soon had most everything under control.

Slowly, quite reluctantly, the other panel members filtered out, including Nancy, who was the last to succumb. We clapped and shimmied and saluted our elders and made everyone on every other floor come out and see just what in the hell we were doing. Some members of other departments even joined us. I laughed and realized this was the perfect time for one of the uptight senators, who made us their whipping boys, to come by and observe the NEA; it would have confirmed all their suspicions.

With all of the arguing, and all of the dancing, and all before lunch, I realized working at the NEA wasn't so bad after all.

33171532R00177

Made in the USA
Middletown, DE
03 July 2016